THE BARBIE KILLER

a novel

Julia McDermott

The Barbie Killer
Red Adept Publishing, LLC
104 Bugenfield Court
Garner, NC 27529
https://RedAdeptPublishing.com/
Copyright © 2026 by Julia McDermott. All rights reserved.

Cover Art by Streetlight Graphics[1]

---

1. http://StreetlightGraphics.com

For Dennis, the one person who knows all my secrets

Chapter 1

Huntington, Kansas
April 1988

The demons had taken over again.

He couldn't control them, and he had given up trying to chase them away a long time ago. He had tried very hard but eventually realized that it was impossible. They lived inside of him all the time. They dwelt there, and when they roused, he was powerless to stop them. He had long wondered if they lived inside anyone else.

He supposed they did because how could they not? There were plenty of psychopaths and sociopaths out there. There were terrorists and mass murderers. He was none of those. Indeed, he had been trained to find people like them and to take them out. Well, not the crazies. But he'd run across more than a few of those. He was the opposite: disciplined, organized, thoughtful, and patient. He was intentional, not random. He liked order and neatness in his home, where he made the rules.

He also had a knack for blending in when he wanted to. When he was young, he hadn't liked that quality, but as an adult, he knew how to use it to his advantage and had learned to appreciate it. Born during the baby boom, he was a typical Midwesterner—a reserved man who did his work and kept to himself. He had worked hard for many years, and he treasured the autonomy and freedom his life afforded him. He was a veteran, a husband, and a father, and he had grown up in Kansas. He enjoyed the outdoors, he liked baseball, and he played golf whenever he could. He loved the trust his family placed in him and the grounding that it gave him to be the man that he was.

Back when he was in the service, the demons had left him alone. Perhaps it was because he was learning so much then—how to stalk people and break into buildings. How to ambush, how to hide, how to torture, and how to kill. And there was little opportunity for a mission back then. But not long after his honorable discharge, the demons started in on him. He was married by then, but that didn't matter. With the passage of time, he had learned to live with the demons. But ever since they'd settled inside him, he had been at their mercy.

Today, he had satisfied them once again. He had stalked her for weeks, following her while she shopped and taking note of her routine. Once he gagged her with duct tape, bound her knees and ankles, and tied her to the bed, the pressure slowly began to subside. Then he was in the midst of it. He didn't particularly enjoy the torture anymore, but it was necessary, and it took time. He had to do it to pacify the demons.

First, he cut away her dress and bra and removed her panties while assuring her that he wouldn't hurt her. He just wanted to look at her, he said, then he would be on his way. He made her hold still, put the doll beside her, and took some Polaroids. Then he started to strangle her with a venetian blind cord, released it and let her breathe, and started again. When he was done and she stopped breathing, he put a plastic bag over her head and felt the familiar rush of release surge within him as he masturbated on her panties.

It was then and only then that he heard the kid crying in the next room.

She'd been so quiet because she hadn't wanted the child to wake up, he realized.

He had to get out of there then—and quickly. He placed a photo of the doll next to her, put the other photos and the doll in his bag, and retraced his steps, double-checking everything. Within a few minutes, he had made sure that he'd left no evidence. Then he saw himself out the back door and crept away. He sighed with relief as he slipped around the corner and got into his vehicle. It was over, and he could go back to living the life that he had so carefully built.

He hadn't had to satisfy the demons in years. Now that he had appeased them, he hoped they would go back to sleep and leave him alone for a while.

Chapter 2

Atlanta, Georgia
January 1995

Dolly stomped into the living room, Tim following right behind her. He closed the door to the kitchen in case the kids, who were playing outside, came in through the back door.

She whirled around to face her husband. "You said that your boss assured you we could stay here and you could work from home. I thought you negotiated that during your interview."

Tim reached for her hand. "He did. But things have changed now. The company is headquartered in Huntington, and I need to be out there and work in the corporate office."

"Can't you push back? I don't want to uproot our family and move to Kansas, Tim. When you took this job, you knew that was a deal-breaker for me."

He shook his head. "I don't want to either, and yes, I did. But I can't go back to my boss with an ultimatum. If I refuse to go, I could lose my job—if not now, then soon. I can't put my job security at risk."

Dolly slumped into a worn blue armchair, and Tim sat down in the matching one next to her. Knowing that he was right didn't make her feel any less indignant.

"Look. I know you're upset, babe," he said. "But the thing is, it's just not practical to live here anymore. I can't do all my work over the phone or fax. I'm part of the investment team, but I'm isolated and out of the loop. I can't be successful this way."

"You could look for another job here in Atlanta," she said.

He shook his head. "It could take months to find anything comparable. You know that."

She did know. Almost a year ago, Tim and everyone in his department had been laid off during a company restructuring that no one saw coming. While he searched for a new position, they had cut expenses, made minimum payments on their credit cards, and lived on severance pay and savings. Dolly, a stay-at-home mother of three, got a part-time job at a department store. After several months of job hunting with no success, Tim started looking for commission-only jobs and considered making a career change for less pay.

Then last fall, a friend and former colleague, Max Buchanan, contacted him about an opening in the department where he worked at Hark Industries and recommended him for the job. Hark was a powerful, well-known oil company as well as the country's second largest privately held firm. The company flew Tim out to Huntington for a series of interviews, and later that week, he got an offer.

Dolly closed her eyes and breathed in deeply. She'd been overjoyed when Tim got the job, but now that there was a huge string attached, she almost felt betrayed.

Tim gently laid his hand on her shoulder and brushed back a lock of her dark-brown hair. His eyes were soft. "Babe, this was just sprung on me too. But even though we'll have to move, I'm happy I have this job. I have to provide for our family, and we need to get back on our feet. And working at headquarters will be a big asset to my career."

Tim's salary at Hark was in the low six figures, and he was on track to earn an annual bonus almost equal to that number.

"I know. I just don't want to leave our life here and start all over a thousand miles away." And she also didn't like it at all when people didn't do what they said they would.

Tim shifted his lanky frame in his chair and rifled a hand through his sandy-brown hair. "We won't be starting over. We'll keep on being us and being a family. And with the money I'll be making, everything will be much easier in Kansas. You'll see. We'll pay off our credit cards and build up our savings again. The cost of living is much lower there, and real estate is a lot cheaper too. We'll be able to afford a bigger house in Huntington than we can here, buy new furniture, and even go on trips with the kids."

Dolly glanced around the small living room. They had bought the furniture in it when they got married fifteen years ago. She'd hoped to replace the armchairs and the faded yellow sofa soon. But it didn't make sense to do that now because they had to sell this home and buy another one. The reality of having to do all that and then pack up their belongings was beginning to sink in. The logistical side of it alone would be a monumental task.

"All of that sounds good and like the right thing to do for our family. But living in a small town in the middle of nowhere—I don't know, Tim. I never imagined it, and I can't now."

"It's not that small, and it's not in the middle of nowhere. It's in central Kansas, two hours north of Oklahoma City. Why don't we look at it as an adventure and focus on the positives, babe? There's a lot less traffic there. The schools are much better, public *and* private—and I was told that Catholic schools are a lot cheaper. There's a lot less crime too. It's a safe place to live."

"Speaking of safety, what about tornadoes?"

He shrugged. "The Midwest is a big place. We probably won't ever see one."

"You don't know that."

"Well, it's very unlikely, and even if it happens, that's what insurance is for. And we won't be living in a trailer park."

"I still say your boss should have told you we'd have to move to Huntington when he offered you the job," Dolly protested. "If we knew then what we know now—"

"I *still* should have taken the job." Tim raised his eyebrows. "I think we would have agreed on that too. But this is how it is, so let's make it work, okay?"

Dolly sighed. "I guess we'll have to."

"Babe, Max moved down there from Kansas City, and he said there are only two real negatives about Huntington," Tim said. "It's as flat as a tabletop, and it's very windy. Not sometimes but almost every day. He said it's a wholesome family-oriented town, though. His wife, Glenda, and their kids love it."

A feeling of resignation began to take root and settle inside of Dolly. She could keep arguing if she wanted to, but she wasn't going to be able to prevent the move from happening.

"How soon do we have to be there?"

Tim's face brightened, his smile broadening as dimples appeared on either side. "The end of the school year. I'm going to have to travel there a lot before then, but over the next few months, we'll have time to get our house ready to sell and then look for one in Huntington. It's going to be a busy time. But things will work out. You'll see."

"I guess you're right. And it won't be forever anyway. At least, I hope not."

"I'm sure it won't. But right now, it's the best thing for us. Believe me."

Dolly started to wrap her head around everything they—mostly, she—would have to do over the next few months. While they got ready to move, she would try to find out more about Huntington so she would know what to expect.

But it would be quite some time before she would discover the town's dark secret.

Chapter 3

Huntington, Kansas
June 1995

When Tim and Dolly Garner and their family arrived in Huntington, Dolly was dozing in the passenger seat, dead tired from their long road trip.

They had gotten up very early that Friday morning and made the journey in one day, Tim doing the driving while Dolly ran herd on the kids. All three nodded off before they were very far outside of metro Atlanta and slept all the way to Birmingham. Stopping for gas and meals made the drive to Huntington take almost sixteen hours. They weren't really a rest-stop family, so Dolly hadn't packed lunches for the trip. They preferred to stop at a McDonald's on the road or anywhere else they found that was fast and cheap.

After they sped through Memphis and crossed over the Mississippi River, the countryside changed dramatically. The land began to flatten out, and the trees were shorter and scruffier, as if struggling to survive and not doing a very good job of it. From there on, nothing Dolly saw reminded her of home. She already missed the tall pines and magnolia trees, the rolling hills, the shady streets, and the dense forest around Atlanta.

That was when it began to hit her. They were far away from home and getting farther. They were really going to live in a nowhere Midwestern town, and she didn't know for how long. She had been so busy preparing for the move that she hadn't had time to learn much about Huntington. During the week before they packed up and headed out of town, she'd said emotional goodbyes to her girlfriends, and they promised to stay in touch with phone calls and letters.

It had been months since they told the kids that they would be moving when school was out. Audrey had lots of friends in kindergarten, but Dolly was sure she would make new ones. She was a typical youngest child, the star of the family and not shy at all, very unlike Dolly as a child. Yet she looked so much like Dolly had at her age, complete with chestnut-brown hair that was just a shade lighter.

However, Dolly was afraid that Hugh and Cole, ages twelve and ten, might find it hard to adjust. Middle school was a tough time to be the new kids in school, but at least they had sports and other activities. Like they had done in the past, she and Tim would sign them up for whatever they wanted to do. Both boys were slim and tall for their ages, and each had a mop of sandy hair like their father's. The two of them got along reasonably well, so at least they would have each other to hang out with initially.

And now, after what seemed like a driving marathon and countless cries of "are we there yet?", they were finally *there*. It was after ten o'clock when Tim pulled up in front of the door to the townhome they would be renting for the summer until their new house was finished and ready for them to move in. The townhome was in the center of a long three-story brick-and-wood building, sandwiched between two identical units on either side. The parking lot was poorly lit, but before Tim turned off the headlights, Dolly saw dark peeling paint on the front door.

"The landlord told me the key would be under the mat," he said as he turned off the engine.

All three kids were now asleep in the back. Tim slid out of the car to grab the key. It wasn't there, and oddly, the door to the unit was unlocked. He walked back to the car, and Dolly rolled down her window.

"Stay here with the kids," Tim told his wife. "I'm going to look around and make sure no one's in there."

"Tim—"

"Don't worry. I'm sure everything's fine. I just want to err on the side of caution. I'll be right back."

Anxious yet annoyed, she rolled up the window and locked the doors. A few minutes later, Tim emerged from the townhome, and Dolly got out of the car.

"It's vacant. The only other entry is a sliding glass door in the basement, and it's locked."

The two of them roused the children from their slumber and ushered them inside.

Audrey rubbed her eyes and looked up. "Where are we, Mommy?"

"We're here," she said, putting an arm around her shoulders. "We're in Kansas, honey."

"Why is it so dark here?"

"It's nighttime," Dolly said, not surprised that Audrey was confused. "It us took all day to get here. We can all go back to sleep in a few minutes."

Cole stumbled over, found the bathroom, and then looked around while Tim and Hugh brought in the suitcases and carried them upstairs. Hugh's eyes were wide as he took in their surroundings, but he said nothing and seemed to move on automatic. The air was warm and musty and reeked of industrial cleaner. Dolly found the thermostat and set it several degrees lower.

She hadn't seen the townhome before. Someone in human resources at Hark had found it a few months ago and showed it to Tim during one of his trips here in the spring. The rooms weren't large, but it had three levels, three bedrooms, and two baths. The movers had already come and gone, and cardboard boxes were stacked everywhere. The workers had assembled the beds, and Dolly had been smart enough to bring sheets, blankets, and pillows in the car as well as a package of toilet paper. She and Tim quickly got the kids' beds ready. All three had been awake most of the day and seemed to want nothing more than to collapse in bed.

After settling them upstairs, Tim and Dolly went down to the kitchen. There were two keys sitting on the counter next to a note from the landlord saying that he'd left the door open because he didn't want to leave the keys in a place where anyone could find them and take them.

"That doesn't make any sense," Dolly said. "'Anyone' could also have opened the unlocked door and come inside."

Tim shrugged. "I agree, but if someone did, they're not here now. I'm too tired to think about it right now anyway."

"Let's find the coffee pot before we turn in," Dolly suggested.

They opened boxes marked *kitchen* until they found the coffee maker. Tim unpacked it and set it up.

He gave her a questioning look. "I'll go out and get coffee and filters first thing in the morning, okay?"

"No need," she said. "I've got them in my bag."

He brightened. "You think of everything, babe."

She smiled, forgetting all about their troubling arrival. Everything would be better tomorrow. "Well, I should have thought to put the coffeepot in the car. You know how I am in the morning if I don't have my coffee." Both of them took it black, so they were all set. "Maybe you could go out and get us something for breakfast in the morning."

"Of course I will." He brushed back a lock of her hair, pulled her to him, and put his arms around her. "Let's hit the sack. We can get started on everything tomorrow."

———————◆———————

They spent the weekend unpacking and getting organized. The townhome's two staircases and the floor of every room except the kitchen and bathrooms were covered with dull beige wall-to-wall carpeting, and the chalky white walls were randomly spotted with grimy smudges. The basement smelled vaguely of mildew and was filled with boxes that didn't need to be opened until they moved into the house.

But by Sunday afternoon, the kitchen cabinets were full, the fridge was stocked, and the washer and dryer were connected. It was going to be a challenge to keep this place clean, but they wouldn't have to do it for long, and they had lived in worse places. Their new neighborhood was only a few miles from Tim's office. His commute would be less than ten minutes.

Over the next several days, while Tim was at work, Dolly tooled around in the minivan, exploring the grid-like town with all three kids in tow. Unlike Atlanta, Huntington was easy to navigate, and it wasn't hard to learn how to get around. The land *was* as flat as a board, without so much as a slight incline anywhere in sight. Straight four-lane roads ran north-south and east-west, their intersections exactly one mile apart. Interstate 35 divided the town in half, and the Arkansas River snaked through the middle of town, flowing south toward the Mississippi. Dolly soon learned that people didn't pronounce the river like the state. Here, they said "are-*kan*-zas," which sounded like "our Kansas" to her southern ear.

One day, after she and the kids got home from the grocery store—a replica of Kroger called Dillons—Dolly spotted a big spider on the linoleum floor in the kitchen. She jumped back and screamed, shaking.

Hugh rushed over to his mom. "What's the matter?"

She pointed at the floor, and he stomped on the spider with his sneaker, killing it. Recovering, Dolly grabbed a paper towel and handed it to him.

"You okay, Mom?"

"Yeah. Thanks, honey. Get it all and whatever's on the bottom of your shoe too."

He did so and threw the paper towel away. She got the Lysol out, hastily cleaned the area, and made a mental note to do the entire kitchen floor later.

"I know we shouldn't kill them," she said, "but I panicked. You know how I am."

"Yeah," he said. "I should have caught it and put it outside."

Dolly let out a deep breath. "Well, I'm glad you did it. It could have been poisonous. And I didn't want that thing running around loose in here. Help me put away the groceries now."

Hugh and his brother and sister knew that she was afraid of bugs and of spiders in particular. Maybe this spider was a one-off that somehow got in while the movers were bringing in boxes. She and Tim had been assured that this townhome had been treated for insects. Dolly planned to use the same pest control company they had in Atlanta in their new home.

After lunch that afternoon, Dolly took the kids with her to a home décor store in the West Side of town where she could pick out wallpaper and tile. Their new neighborhood and Tim's office were in the East Side, where professionals, executives, and white-collar workers lived, according to the realtor and Tim's co-workers. The East Side was filled with nice neighborhoods and was dotted with private golf courses. The West Side was home to blue-collar workers who lived in modest wood houses, apartment complexes, and trailer parks. Both sides were home to plenty of chain restaurants and fast-food places, and both featured an aging one-story mall anchored by a Sears and a Dillard's. When a Gap store held its grand opening in an East Side strip shopping center a few weeks earlier, it had been front-page news in *The Huntington Post*.

During the next several days, as Dolly and the children cruised around town, they rarely saw a police car, so she assumed crime was low and that the town didn't need many cops.

It must be a safe place to live.

Chapter 4

Tim's first week at corporate headquarters went relatively well. Fitting into a new company could be stressful, and he tried to be observant and to learn as much as possible about office dynamics. Within days, he felt as if he had stepped into the job without missing a beat.

Max's office was a few doors down from Tim's, and their boss, Joe Walton, had a corner office. His commute was the shortest he'd ever had, and so far, he hadn't noticed much traffic or anything resembling a rush hour. Max had been as right about that as he had been about many other aspects of life in Huntington. Housing *was* a lot less expensive. A new home would have cost three times as much in Atlanta. The Garners would have a much bigger backyard than their previous one, so the kids would have a lot of room to play. There was even a park and a baseball diamond down the street, in the center of the neighborhood.

What Max had reported as the only negatives—the constant wind and the level terrain—Tim saw as positives. It was a great place to fly kites and to ride bikes. Traveling here on business over the spring, he had formed a good impression of Huntington in general, and he liked the people, who seemed no-nonsense and hardworking. Like Joe, they said what they meant, and in Tim's view, that was a good attribute in a boss.

He, Max, and everybody who wasn't away on business ate lunch every day at the Hark company cafeteria in the basement. On Friday, Tim took the elevator down with Max.

"How are you settling in?" Max asked when the door closed. Max was older than Tim but was in shape and had thinning brown hair and a squarish, nondescript face.

"Pretty well. Being here in the office makes a big difference."

"How is your wife doing with the move? And the children?"

Tim tilted his head. "They're adjusting, I guess. Kids are resilient, and Dolly, well, she'll come around in time. Especially once our new house is finished."

Max nodded. "Oh, I forgot you were having one built. We did too. Glenda didn't like leaving Kansas City, but after we moved into it, she was a lot happier. She's made lots of friends over the last six months too."

The door opened on the basement floor, and they ambled over to the counter, where their choices included burgers, sandwiches, and fresh salads. The aroma of fries and bacon was pervasive.

"I hope Dolly will do the same," Tim said.

"By the way, we need to get out to the golf course soon." Max grinned.

Tim glanced at him, grabbed a club sandwich, and put it on his tray. "I'd love to," he said, smiling. "Just give me a couple of weeks to get a kitchen pass."

He wouldn't be asking for a green light from Dolly to spend a Saturday playing golf just yet. There was too much going on at home, and he knew she was stressed. But he had already looked into private golf courses and was itching to play. Country clubs were quite expensive in Atlanta, so they hadn't belonged to one there. Some clubs here were pricey, too, but some had a low initiation fee and low monthly fees. Several of Tim and Max's colleagues were members of a club called Ardennes. For Hark executives, the fee to join was only a thousand dollars, so Tim thought it was a good buy and that he and Dolly should become members.

⸺●⸺

Within weeks, Dolly and the kids settled into a summer routine. Each morning they went to a fitness center they had recently joined called the Athletic Club. They'd been members of the local YM-

CA in Atlanta, but the branch here was much older, smaller and had a lot less to offer. The Athletic Club was a private fitness club that had large indoor and outdoor pools, state-of-the-art exercise equipment, and a dozen tennis courts.

Each day, Dolly dropped Audrey off at the nursery, and Cole and Hugh played basketball in the gym while she did a step aerobics class or used the weight machines. If it was hot outside—and the high was often over a hundred degrees—they usually went home for lunch and then back to the outdoor pool for the afternoon. About once a week, she hit the easy button and took the kids to McDonald's to pick up burgers for the boys, a Happy Meal for Audrey, and a tasteless salad for herself. Happy Meals came with colorful stuffed Beanie Babies, the newest craze, and Audrey was amassing a large collection of them. The more it grew, the more the boys griped that she always got what she wanted whereas they didn't.

One morning, Dolly arrived early at the Athletic Club for step class. As she hovered next to the locked studio door, she couldn't help but overhear two women talking nearby. She glanced at them then looked away and pretended to look for something in her purse. She didn't want to eavesdrop, but they were talking so loudly that she had no choice.

Though she'd been coming to this class for a few weeks, she hadn't met very many people here—or elsewhere, for that matter. People might nod or say hi, but they didn't engage in conversation with a stranger. But she had the feeling she'd seen these women before and not necessarily in this class. However, in the fishbowl that was Huntington, it wasn't unusual to see the same people almost everywhere one went. Flying under the radar was virtually impossible since, though not tiny, Huntington was smaller than lots of suburbs. And it was isolated. Once you were outside the town limits, you weren't anywhere.

You were nowhere.

"No, I'm telling you, Shelly," the taller woman said, her voice becoming shrill. She was fortyish and slim, and her short blond hair topped a narrow, pinched face. "When he did that, it destroyed *every good feeling* I've ever had for him. Now, I have nothing but *hate* in my heart for that man."

Despite Dolly's intention not to listen, her ears pricked as she wondered what "that man" had done.

"Come on, Barb," said Shelly. "He can't be that bad."

A petite brunette with bulging eyes capped by pencil-thin eyebrows, Shelly had makeup on and was decked out in designer workout attire. She reminded Dolly of women she knew in Atlanta who spent more time getting ready to go to the gym than they did working out.

"Oh, but he *is*. You have no idea, Shelly. I promise."

At that moment, the class instructor, a short and perky young woman with a dirty-blond ponytail and a deep tan, rushed by and unlocked the door to the studio.

"Good morning, ladies!" she said. "Come on in!"

Dolly waited for Barb and Shelly to enter ahead of her. Neither one moved.

"After y'all," she said, gesturing toward the studio and immediately regretting having said "y'all" instead of "you." This was Kansas, not Georgia, after all, and although she thought she didn't have a strong southern accent, she felt self-conscious about having used that word.

Barb had a startled look on her face, and Shelly's eyes were wide. *Surely, they've heard the word y'all before. Or—do they know I was eavesdropping? Are they embarrassed—or angry?*

"No, no, after you," Barb said, still motionless. Her lips were pressed in a thin line.

Dolly smiled weakly, walked into the room, and claimed a spot near the front. Barb and Shelly found spaces right next to each other in the back. Dolly decided that she would say hello to them after class and introduce herself. If they realized that she'd overheard them talking, what difference did it make anyway?

The music began. Dolly did her best to follow the instructor for the next fifty minutes. She was dripping with sweat when class wrapped up with a cooldown and stretches. Then she picked up her platform, went to put it away, and noticed that Barb and Shelly were gone.

Dolly was on the way to the gym to get the boys when she saw a woman about her age walking right toward her and who looked as if she recognized her.

"Hello, there," the woman said, stopping in front of Dolly and wearing a smile that was reflected in her sparkling dark eyes. Her hair was pulled back in a ponytail. "I feel like I've seen you somewhere recently. Maybe at something Hark-related?"

Dolly shrugged. "A cocktail party?" She and Tim recently had gone to one where he'd introduced her to some of his colleagues and their wives.

The woman nodded. "Yeah, that sounds right. I'm Heidi Barron."

"Dolly Garner." She smiled.

Heidi's brows shot up. "Dolly? Like in Dolly Parton?"

Dolly blushed. "Guilty."

Heidi drew her head back a little as her eyes widened. "Well, hello, Dolly. Tell me, is it your real name?"

She shook her head. She'd been asked this question countless times. "It's Dorothy. But I've been called Dolly ever since I can remember."

Heidi cocked her head, still amused but in a good way. "Dorothy in Kansas! How *apropos*."

Dolly shrugged again. "There's no place like home. Although it doesn't really feel like home yet."

"You're new in town?" Heidi asked. She was a couple inches taller than Dolly, who at five feet eight was more used to meeting women who were shorter than she was.

"We moved here from Atlanta at the end of June."

"We were transferred from Houston two years ago," Heidi said, her tone revealing a touch of commiseration. "You have kids?"

Dolly nodded. "Two boys and a girl."

"Me too! How old are they?" Heidi asked.

"Twelve, ten, and six. My daughter's the youngest."

"My boys are fourteen and twelve, and my little girl is seven!" Heidi said, elated.

The ice broken, they chatted on and learned they had other things in common. Both were currently stay-at-home moms. Their children went to different private schools, but Heidi's younger son was a Boy Scout, and so were Cole and Hugh. Heidi's husband, Matt, was in shipping at Hark and didn't cross paths with Tim, who was in the bonds department.

"Where do you live?" Heidi asked. "What neighborhood?"

"We're renting a townhouse on Stockton Road while our house is being built. It's in the Glenlake subdivision. It should be finished soon."

Heidi smiled again. "That's *our* neighborhood." Then she drew her head back and narrowed her eyes, keeping them trained on Dolly. "Wait. Did you guys buy that last vacant lot over on Lakewood Drive?"

"We did. Why?"

Since it was in the heart of the subdivision, Dolly had thought it odd that it sold last. But many people preferred to be on cul-de-sacs, and some liked the privacy of a lot on the edge of the neighborhood. And builders sold every lot, including the last one.

Heidi hesitated for a second before replying. Her eyes widened, and she shook her head. "Oh, no reason. We're over on Meadow Lane. So, how do you like Huntington?"

"I'm adjusting," Dolly said. "Honestly, it feels strange living in a much smaller city."

"I know. You'll get used to it, though. What do you think about the people?"

Dolly shrugged. "I don't know. I guess they're nice, but they're not like Southerners."

Heidi laughed. "That's for sure. They're different, and sometimes, they can be a little cold. But you'll get used to them too. I promise."

Dolly had noticed that people here walked around as if they had blinders on, rarely making eye contact with others. She hadn't seen anyone hold a door open for someone else or say hello to a stranger.

"I felt the same way when we arrived," Heidi continued. "People here are kind of private. They keep to themselves. They're Midwesterners—at least, they'll say they are even though this is technically the prairie. America's Heartland. They're not exactly like Upper Midwesterners, but they speak with a Midwestern twang. But once you get to know them, they can actually be friendly."

Dolly cocked her head. "That's good to know, I guess."

Heidi looked quickly to her right and left before locking eyes with Dolly and quietly adding, "You *do* know that the East Side is the unofficial Hark company enclave, don't you?"

"Yeah. I mean, so I've heard. We've never really lived near people Tim works with."

"Well, let me tell you, there's a whole social stratum of Hark executives—mostly men—and their families living within a five-mile radius of each other. Probably *less* than five miles." Her brows shot up. "It can be weird."

"Oh?" Dolly managed to say.

Heidi nodded. "I mean, there are other people who live there too. It's where doctors, lawyers, and other professionals live. But the vast majority work for Hark, and lots are transfers."

This was exactly what Tim's boss had told him. Glenlake, their subdivision, and those nearby were filled with Hark employees. Even the CEO, Peter Hark, lived nearby. But word was that he lived in a modest home on a large piece of property that was enclosed by a tall wood fence, keeping it hidden from the public. However, he was building a massive lodge in Aspen, complete with a helicopter pad and an airplane runway.

"It makes sense to live so close to the office, I guess," Dolly said. "Tim had a thirty-minute commute in Atlanta. And that was with no traffic."

"Right. But it's kind of strange living next door to and around the corner from every Tom, Dick, and Harry—and the occasional Harriett—that Matt works with. It's part of the culture, though. Not the Midwestern one, I mean. The Hark one."

"Hmm. Adjusting to that could be a challenge for me." And it could be awkward at times.

Dolly felt surprised at herself for being so candid with a woman she'd just met. However, this was the first time she felt she could be open with someone who lived here, and it felt good.

"It was quite challenging for me," Heidi admitted. "You'll see Hark executives all over the place, whether you know it or not. And lots of their wives, often dressed to kill. Even if they're just going to Dillons."

Dolly raised her eyebrows again.

Heidi did the same then whispered, "Don't worry. It's not as Stepford Wives-ish as it sounds."

Dolly drew in a breath. Heidi had just nailed Dolly's first impression of lots of women, possibly Hark wives, that she had seen around town. They were polished, attractive, and put-together, never harried or stressed out. And they were always dressed up, looking as if they wouldn't be caught dead in sweats or without their makeup on. They were poised yet uptight, like ballet dancers who were much more tense than they were in sync.

Like women who share a secret.

"That said," Heidi continued, "they're all about having perfect children, ideal husbands, and immaculate homes. They're kind of uptight and very buttoned-up—even more than the typical Midwesterner, if you ask me. It's like they're wearing a mask that they never take off."

Now Dolly was surprised at Heidi's candor. Evidently, Heidi wasn't like the women she'd described—or thought she wasn't—but having just met Dolly, how did she know Dolly wasn't like them—at least a little bit?

Because, just like Heidi, I don't wear makeup or designer workout clothes to the gym. And because, even though our personalities are different, we're both friendly and approachable.

"Thanks for the heads-up," Dolly said, "and it's good to know I wasn't imagining things. I've noticed women who seemed that way and figured they had their own clique or something."

Heidi pressed her lips together and nodded. "You're right—and some of them live in our neighborhood. But we have lots of normal neighbors too. Do you want to meet a few of them? And do you like to read?"

"I'd love to, and yes, I do."

"Good. There's a book club that meets every month at someone's house. Would you like to go to our next meeting with me? I'll pick you up."

"That would be great, and thanks! What's the book?"

"*To Die Unmourned* by Carla McCreedy. It doesn't matter if you don't read it. It's mostly just about getting together and drinking wine."

"Sounds wonderful. I'll look for the book, though."

Chapter 5

The following week, Heidi picked Dolly up for book club just as Tim and the children sat down for dinner.

"Have fun, babe," he said.

She grabbed her purse. "See you later."

She hurried out the door and climbed into Heidi's white SUV. Five minutes later, they arrived at Celeste Townsend's door, and Heidi introduced Dolly to her.

"Nice to meet you," Celeste said. She was a short woman with chin-length dark hair and a fringe of bangs camouflaging a lined forehead. She ushered Heidi and Dolly to the kitchen and motioned toward the wine bottles and glasses sitting on the counter.

"Please help yourselves," she said.

As Dolly poured a glass of pinot grigio, she smelled a hint of Pine-Sol in the air and noted that the room was spotless.

Celeste turned to the group of ladies gathered around the island, many of whom had stopped chatting and were looking at Dolly. "Everybody, this is Dolly Garner."

Dolly said hello and managed to remember a few names before she gave up trying. Over the next half hour, she learned that everybody except Heidi had grown up in Huntington or elsewhere in Kansas. Some of their kids went to private school and some to public.

"Do you miss Atlanta, Dolly?" Celeste asked.

Dolly paused for a moment before answering. "I do miss it, and I really miss my friends there. I don't miss the traffic, though. Or the crime."

"Does Atlanta have a lot of crime?" Celeste asked.

"It's a big city. We lived in a suburb, but you had to be careful."

"We don't have any crime in Huntington," Celeste said.

A redhead named Betsy wearing jeans and tortoiseshell glasses spun around and faced her. "That's not really true, Celeste."

"I don't know," Celeste said. "I've lived here all my life, and I've *never* worried about crime."

"I grew up in Bonneville, and *I* have," a slender woman named Susie with silky long blond hair added. Dolly had learned that Bonneville was a little community south of Huntington, close enough to be considered a sort of suburb. "Don't you or Bob worry about break-ins, Celeste?"

She shrugged. "Not at all. I mean, Bob's got a gun, but we leave our doors unlocked during the day and our windows open. He doesn't even lock up his shed."

Everyone stared at her, and no one said anything for a moment. Then Betsy broke the silence.

"It's good that you feel so safe," she said in a hushed tone. "But ever since that girl was brutally murdered in the sixties, I haven't. We keep our doors and windows locked."

"What girl?" Dolly asked.

The room was silent for a few seconds, and some women looked down at the floor. Then Betsy turned to Dolly. "Back then," she said, "the land where our neighborhood is was rural. It was part of Huntington, but it was really out in the sticks. There were only a few small houses on it. The girl lived in one of them. One night, a boy from her high school broke into her bedroom and slashed her throat."

"No one knows that for sure, Betsy. But that's the story that went around," Celeste said. "People have been gossiping about it ever since, but no one saw who did it."

"*Somebody* did it," said Betsy.

"Were her parents at home? Did they ever catch the killer?" Dolly asked.

"They *were* home, but they didn't hear him," Betsy said. "Whoever it was must have done it real fast. And no, the killer was never found."

"Why not?"

"No one knows," Susie put in, shaking her head. "Somehow, the killer got away. Her parents put their house on the market but couldn't sell it. Eventually, the bank foreclosed on it, and all the neighbors moved away."

"Fast forward to about seven years ago," Betsy said. "Some builders came in, bought up all the land, and developed our subdivision. The house where she was murdered was right in the middle of it."

"Where, exactly?" Dolly asked.

Several women exchanged glances.

"On your lot," said Heidi quietly.

Dolly's eyes widened. "Oh my God." No wonder Heidi had reacted that way when Dolly told her which lot they had bought. "That's horrible."

"Don't worry about it, Dolly," Heidi said. "I mean, it was so long ago. We live in the middle of the Great Plains. No one knows what happened out here before our time. And we don't really need to know."

"*Some* people knew what happened on our lot, though. Like our builder and our real estate agent."

"If they did, you can't really blame them for not telling you," Heidi said. "It might have upset you if they had, but it wouldn't have changed anything. You probably still would have bought it and built your home on it."

"I think I *can* blame them," Dolly said, "and I'm not at all sure we would have." With a glass of wine in her system and her dander up, she forged on. "It definitely would have upset me, and I'm not happy that we didn't know. If we'd known, we might have kept looking."

"Well, in any case," Celeste said, "you can't rewrite the past. None of us can. And I'm with Heidi." She glanced at Heidi and looked back at Dolly, lowering her chin. "We don't need to know everything that happened in the past. And blame gets you nowhere. Believe me."

Everyone was silent while Celeste and Dolly locked eyes for a few seconds. Then Celeste turned to the group and smiled. "Now, shall we go into the den and talk about the book?"

Chapter 6

When Dolly got home around ten thirty that night, Tim was in bed reading. She quickly undressed, changed into her black nightgown, and slid in next to him.

"How was it?" He turned toward her and put his book down. "Did you have fun?"

"I did," she said, her tone indicating slight surprise. "And I met a lot of neighbors."

"Good. Are they nice?"

"Yeah," she said, "they're very nice. The hostess, Celeste, is a little odd, though."

Tim raised his eyebrows. "What do you mean?"

"Well, while we were in the kitchen talking, before we started discussing the book, she said that she leaves her doors unlocked during the day, and she never worries about crime."

"Well, this *is* Huntington. Maybe a lot of people do that."

"Yeah. But then she said they have a gun."

"Maybe that's why she doesn't worry about crime," he said.

"But then another woman said she worries about it—about things like break-ins."

Tim bit his lip and then said, "Well, either one's a worrier and the other one isn't, or there've been a rash of break-ins here recently."

"Exactly. No one said there had been, but that led to someone else telling a grim story from thirty years ago about something that happened on our property."

"Go on," Tim said, intrigued.

Dolly repeated the story, finishing up by emphasizing the fact that their home was being built on the spot where the unsolved murder had been committed.

"That's pretty creepy. But I think I agree with your friend Heidi. Since it happened such a long time ago, I don't think we should waste our time thinking about it."

"But the killer was never found. It just seems disturbing. Plus, wouldn't you have wanted to know about it before we decided to build our house there?"

Tim slid his arm around her shoulders. "I don't know. I mean, it does sound chilling. But it could be the last time a murder happened in this town."

She snuggled up next to him and stretched her legs. "Maybe. But I can't help but wonder if it means our property is, I don't know, cursed or something."

Tim gave her a measured look and narrowed his eyes. "I didn't know you believed in curses."

She propped up on her elbows and turned on her side toward him. "I'm not sure if I do or not. But knowing that a murder took place there is making me look at it differently because it's part of its history. History that can't be rewritten."

"But how would that affect us? Or anyone else, for that matter?"

"I don't know. But what if the killer still lives somewhere around here? What if, now that a new house is being built here, he decides to come back to the scene of the crime?"

"I think you're overthinking this. Plus, given how long it's been, that seems pretty unlikely to me. He's probably dead by now." He gently laid a hand on Dolly's arm. "And whatever happened, as you say, there's nothing we can do about it now. I'm sure we'll be safe. *We* keep our doors locked, and we'll have a security system too."

Dolly gave him a kiss and lay back down. "I guess you're right. I'm going to sleep."

Tim picked up his book but couldn't focus. *What if finding out about that murder triggers her to walk in her sleep?*

She hadn't done that in a good while, but just when it seemed like she'd stopped doing it for good, she did it again. Afterward, she never remembered what she did in her sleep, but they usually figured it out. She'd done a load of laundry, or she'd cleaned the fridge or reorganized the pantry. But she had never done anything dangerous or crazy, like drive away or jump out of a window. However, he was afraid that one night, she might—which was why, over the years, he had become a light sleeper. If she stirred, he almost always drew closer to her in bed.

But he was troubled about Dolly's preoccupation with the unsolved murder and fixation about curses. Dolly had just met these women, and she didn't really know them. Heidi was fine, but Celeste sounded like a strange bird. As for not being concerned about crime, Tim figured she must have her reasons for that and for owning a gun. Perhaps he should ask Max or Roger about whether there *had* been some break-ins lately. In any case, Celeste was entitled to her own views, her own decisions, and her own level of comfort. As were they.

⸻ ◉ ⸻

The next morning at the office, Tim's boss handed him an invitation to a pool party for the whole department, to be held the following Saturday at his home.

"It's a yearly thing we do," Joe said with a nod. Joe was fiftyish, from Huntington, and had been with Hark since he was in his twenties. He was a tall man with gray hair and steely eyes. "Hope you and your wife can attend."

"Thanks, Joe," Tim said. "I'm sure she would love to come."

Thirty minutes later, Tim met with Roger Stillwell, the corporate attorney for the group. Roger was at least a dozen years older, but he was fit and had more hair than most other men his age. He was also from Huntington and had been with Hark for many years. Tim and

Roger had developed a cordial relationship working together since Tim had joined the company, and Roger was highly regarded and well respected at Hark. Tim entered the small conference room to find him waiting with a young guy that Tim had seen before but hadn't met.

"Tim, this is Jake Miller," Roger said. "Jake, meet Tim Garner. Tim started a few months ago and just moved here from Atlanta."

The two men shook hands. Jake was tall and wiry with a fresh face and a head full of blond hair.

"Good to meet you, Jake."

"Pleased to meet you, and welcome to Kansas, sir," Jake said.

"Thank you."

Roger added, "Jake graduated from the University of Kansas in May. He started about a month ago and has been helping me out lately. Hope you don't mind that I asked him to sit in."

"Not at all," Tim said, smiling. "Isn't it Rock Chalk, Jayhawk, K-U?" Many of their colleagues went to Kansas and often chatted about sports. Tim had paid attention when they did.

Jake grinned. "Very good, sir. And yes, it is. When we're winning."

"No need for 'sir,'" Roger said to him. "Unless you're talking to Peter Hark, that is."

"Yes, sir. I mean, understood." Jake's face colored a little.

Roger smiled, and they all sat down at the table to discuss a deal Tim was working on. Five minutes later, a brunette dressed in a dark skirt and matching jacket knocked on the door, opened it, and poked her head in.

"Sorry to disrupt your meeting, Roger," she said, her accent decidedly Midwestern with its nasal twang. "Wanted to remind you about your lunch with Carter Brooks today."

"Thank you," he said. "Tim, this is Tamara Weeks. She's a secretary in the legal department and does a great job keeping me on track." He winked at her, his eyes sparkling. "Not just me, though. She helps all of us in the department."

"Nice to meet you, Tamara," Tim said.

"Tim—?"

"Garner," Roger said.

"Likewise, Mr. Garner," Tamara said.

"Anything else, Tamara?" Roger asked.

"That's all for now," she said, her voice clipped. "Let me know if you need anything."

"Will do," Roger said as she closed the door. "It's important to stay on her good side," he said with a smirk.

The meeting wrapped up in less than a half hour, and Roger sent Jake on his way to do some research.

"So," Roger said, turning toward Tim, "not sure if I've already said this, but if you have any questions about how things are done here, don't hesitate to ask."

"Thanks, and I won't." They stood up and started toward the door.

"Looks like someone already advised you that it's business attire at the office," Roger said, glancing at Tim's conservative navy suit and dark tie. "We don't do business casual."

"Suits me fine," he said, smiling. "I'm glad I don't have to figure out what to wear."

Roger chuckled, and they lingered by the door. "I know what you mean. It's a lot easier to stick to clothes that we already own. You'll find that things are straightforward here but pretty formal too."

"Oh? In what way?" Tim lifted his brows.

"Well, we use Robert's Rules of Order in department meetings, for one thing. You're familiar with that, I suppose?"

"Of course." His previous employer didn't use them, but the one before that did.

"We're traditional but not complicated. We respect each other's autonomy and freedom to make decisions."

Tim would wait and see if he shared that view. But he was happy to know it was Roger's.

"And we're not pretentious," Roger continued. "You'll often see Peter Hark waiting in line for lunch in the employee cafeteria along with everyone else."

Tim hadn't seen him down there so far, but he found the idea of it surprising and a little intriguing. "Joe told me that he's brilliant and very cerebral."

Roger nodded. "Went to MIT on a scholarship, served in the army, and been running the company since the early seventies. But you'd never know he's a billionaire. Drives an old car, isn't flashy, and is reportedly quite frugal. I'm told he likes to work with his hands. A quiet, unassuming guy and very reserved. Married with two kids and likes to keep a low profile and fly under the radar." He grinned. "You'll see."

Chapter 7

Back in February, Hark had flown Tim and Dolly to Huntington one weekend to look for a house. After touring one home after another and vetoing them all, they had decided to build a house instead. Dolly had been thankful that, rather than settling for a house she didn't want, they could customize a new one. Now, it was late July, and the house would be finished in a month or so.

One evening, she went to a parents' meeting at the kids' new school while Tim stayed home with them. All three would be attending St. Thomas More Catholic School in the fall, and tonight's topic was a new reading program for middle schoolers. Dolly found a chair in the back of the room and sat down.

The principal welcomed everyone, introduced the teachers sitting behind her, and the meeting began. Dolly looked around, wondering which moms here had children who would be in seventh grade with Hugh. After a short speech, the principal asked an English teacher to play a video explaining the new program. Dolly noticed that the accents of the people in the video were much stronger than those of most residents of Huntington. Near the end of it, others who spoke with a strong Southern accent endorsed the reading program, and Dolly heard people around her chuckling and giggling. She felt annoyed and a little self-conscious even though she hadn't opened her mouth, but then, where she was from, she knew the reverse might happen. She crossed her arms in front of her and made a mental note to pay attention to her pronunciation.

After the video, there was a question-and-answer session, and lots of parents raised their hands. Dolly waited several minutes and then lifted hers.

"Yes, in the back," said the principal, pointing to her.

"I just moved here from Atlanta," Dolly began, standing up and enunciating as well as she could. "Our Catholic school's reading program there for middle schoolers was different. The kids didn't get points for pages read like they do in this one. It was more focused on comprehension and doing book reports—getting the kids to *digest* what they read."

Before she had a chance to continue and ask about the objectives of this program, the principal cut her off with a wave of her hand. "Welcome to Huntington and to St. Thomas More. While I'm glad you had a reading program in your old school, I think you'll find this one to be excellent. It will incentivize the students to read more for pleasure and outside of school. Next question?"

Dolly sat down and slumped back in her seat, feeling unheard and like she'd been brushed off. She glanced around again and noticed a couple of moms looking at her, their faces stony. No one offered a smile. They must have tagged her as another newcomer who had lamely tried to inject "the way we did it back home" into the discussion.

Okay. You—and Hugh—will just have to do things the way they do them here.

She clasped her hands and bit her lip. Were any of these mothers married to Hark executives? Some were dressed very nicely and not in business clothes. Dolly didn't have sweats on, but she wasn't wearing an outfit that she would go out to dinner in, like they were.

Don't be so judgmental. Maybe they are going out after. You don't know them anyway.

The meeting dragged on, and when it was over, instead of introducing herself to anyone, Dolly slipped out the door and walked to her car. Despite her intention not to think about it, she began to wonder if any of them knew about the long-ago murder of the teenage girl. As she drove back to the townhome, she couldn't get the story and the way she had learned of it out of her mind.

The next day, she considered calling the realtor to ask if she knew about the murder and whether such a thing was supposed to be disclosed to the buyer. But instead of doing that, Dolly took the kids with her to the public library and did some research while they looked for books. With the librarian's help, she discovered that if a homicide had occurred inside a home in the state of Kansas, the seller was legally required to disclose it. If a violent crime had occurred in it, they weren't, though, and if a murder had taken place in a house that had once stood on a vacant lot, that, too, didn't have to be disclosed.

She and Tim had gotten their lot for a song, according to the realtor, and that had allowed them to afford upgrades like hardwood floors, specialty tile, and custom cabinets. At the time, Dolly thought that it was priced so low because the builder wanted to finish up in the subdivision and move on. But maybe the real reason it was on sale was because of its tragic history. Like the site of a string of businesses that had all gone bankrupt, their land had bad karma because the prior home was tainted by murder and lost to a foreclosure. Although she didn't wish the lot had cost them more, the possibility that they had inadvertently taken advantage of and profited from the misfortune and suffering of others deeply troubled her.

Could it bring bad luck? Or did it mean that one day they would have to pay?

Chapter 8

Dolly and Tim left Hugh in charge of his brother and sister while they went to the pool party at Joe's house. Joe, his wife, Diane, and their two children, both of whom were a little older than Hugh, lived outside of town about halfway between the Garners' house and Ardennes, the golf club Tim and Dolly had recently joined.

A valet met them in the circular driveway in front of Joe's massive stone house, and as they walked toward the front door, Tim spied Max and Glenda Buchanan standing on the steps. Dolly had met both of them at a company function in Atlanta a while back. Max was wearing a blue polo shirt and khakis—similar to Tim's choice of clothing for this occasion—and Glenda, a tall, willowy blonde, wore a sundress. The Garners said hello to them in the spacious foyer.

"Great to see you, Dolly!" Glenda exclaimed. "How do you like Huntington so far?"

"So nice to see you as well," said Dolly, her eyes sparkling as she returned Glenda's smile. "It's growing on me."

Tim smiled when her heard her say that as he shook hands with Max and greeted Glenda. He thought Dolly looked beautiful in her light-blue sleeveless dress.

"Would you look at this place?" Glenda half whispered to Dolly. "What a *palace*!"

"It's amazing," Dolly murmured, impressed by the high ceilings and Oriental rugs.

Tim couldn't help but note the exquisite marble flooring and expensive furnishings in Joe's home. He had never seen a house like this. It felt more like a boutique hotel, complete with bouquets of fresh flowers on every surface and artwork in ornate gold frames covering the walls.

The two couples ambled down a wide corridor and into an enormous open room with floor-to-ceiling windows. A large pool was in the center of the courtyard, surrounded by colorful parasol umbrella tables and lounge chairs and ringed by luscious pink flowering shrubs. A white garden shed was visible several yards to the left. There was a big white tent at the far end of the pool, shading a long table filled with platters of food. Servers roamed around the deck, offering *hors d'oeuvres* to guests, and a line was forming at the bar.

"Max said your house is almost ready," Glenda said to Dolly. "How exciting! I bet you can't wait to move in."

Dolly smiled. "I'm counting the days," she said. Packing up again would be a chore, but she was tired of living in the rental, and her concerns about the lot's history had begun to fade. "I can't wait for school to start too. The kids have been going a little nuts lately."

"Mine too," Glenda said in a low tone, nodding. "I'm really looking forward to getting back into a routine."

Tim and Max finished chatting, and Tim suggested they go get a drink. They strolled outside toward the bar, and Dolly noticed that everyone at the party was dressed casually but tastefully. The baking August heat had become oppressive, and she would be glad when it abated. The sparkling blue water in the pool reflected the bright sunlight, and vapor rose from its surface. Tim ordered a white wine for Dolly and a beer for himself, and within minutes, they were surrounded by a cadre of people from his department.

A few minutes later, they made their way back inside. Tim spied Joe across the room, talking to Roger, and Joe smiled and waved at him as they approached. Then Joe looked back at Roger, whose back was to Tim.

"We should discuss that privately," Tim heard Joe say to Roger.

Roger turned around and gave Dolly a slight double take. As Tim introduced her, he wondered if Roger had seen her somewhere, maybe out shopping. If so, he hadn't mentioned it.

"Delighted to meet you, Dolly," Joe said.

"Likewise," Roger said. "She's gorgeous, Tim. I'd say you're a very lucky man."

Dolly blushed slightly as Tim beamed wordlessly at her. However, she felt like Roger had just complimented not her but something Tim owned, like a sports car or a luxury watch. Before Tim could respond, a very attractive brunette appeared out of nowhere, walked up to Roger, and took his arm.

"Hello, darling," Roger said. "Dolly and Tim Garner, this is my lovely wife, Mary Ellen."

"Pleased to meet you both," she said with a smile that seemed natural yet forced.

Is she one of the "cliquey" Hark wives that Heidi mentioned?

Everyone began chatting, and in a few moments, the women were carrying on their own conversation and the men theirs. Dolly began to feel at ease and let go of what she now thought of as rash—and perhaps irrational—judgments of both Roger and Mary Ellen.

Tim kept quiet more than he spoke and focused on listening. That strategy had worked well while he was trying to learn the ropes of a new company and its culture. He was still feeling his way when it came to personalities at Hark, and while he was at the office, it seemed easier to stay quiet. There, he only had to be productive and efficient, but here, he had to socialize and make an effort to be charming. He wasn't awful at that, but he wasn't a natural either. It was hard for him to be social when he was *on*—playing a part, somewhat on guard, and slightly afraid of committing a *faux pas*. However, realizing that others might be feeling the somewhat same way, he relaxed a bit. Dolly seemed to be enjoying herself, and that and her presence here were a big help.

Joe and Roger drifted away and began talking to a young junior executive who had recently joined the company. Tim had seen the guy around, but he didn't work with him, and they hadn't been formally introduced. The three men formed a tight circle and edged away, so his opportunity to meet the man and to participate in the *tête-à-tête* vanished. Tim reached for Dolly's elbow and signaled his desire to extricate himself from the group and to take her with him to go elsewhere and mingle.

During the next twenty minutes, they talked to some of Tim's co-workers and their spouses as everyone nibbled on appetizers. Then Roger and Mary Ellen came up to them, and she took Dolly's arm.

"Let me introduce you to some ladies you should meet, Dolly. See you boys later."

She led Dolly away as she waved goodbye to Roger and Tim. Dolly kept her eye out for Heidi but then remembered that she wouldn't be here because Matt worked in a different department. This gathering was for Joe's group only.

They walked up to two impeccably dressed women with flawless hair and makeup who were standing in a shady spot.

"Jan and Connie, meet Dolly," Mary Ellen said. "She's new to town, and her husband works with Roger." She turned to Dolly. "Both of their husbands have been at Hark a long time."

After they said, "Nice to meet you," Dolly had the impression that Jan and Connie were evaluating her outfit, shoes, and bag. Both carried expensive designer purses, and their diamond bracelets set off perfectly manicured, polished nails. Mary Ellen's attire was similar but less showy. Dolly felt her more natural look was subpar in comparison, if not inferior.

"So, tell Dolly and me what you've both been up to lately," Mary Ellen said.

Jan's lips formed a smile that her eyes didn't reflect, and Connie's face was expressionless and her eyes wide and unblinking. She watched Dolly as Jan spoke.

"Nothing new, really," Jan said. "Playing golf whenever it's not scorching hot. And shopping when it is."

"Oh, what are your favorite stores here?" Dolly asked. "I'm so busy with the kids that I don't have much time to shop, so I need some rec-ommendations."

A second passed as the three other women looked at each other and then began giggling.

"Oh, Dolly," said Mary Ellen as the laughter faded. "We don't shop here in Huntington."

"Unless you like Dillard's. Or the Gap," Connie said, her tone sar-castic.

"I haven't laughed that much in a while," Jan said.

Mary Ellen took Dolly's arm and said quietly, "We shop in New York—or in Dallas, at Neiman's. None of the stores in Huntington car-ry anything that's really nice."

Dolly was embarrassed, but she recovered quickly with a weak smile. "Good to know, so thanks. Not sure when I'll be able to make it to either city for a shopping trip," she said sincerely then realized that she must have sounded snarky and immediately regretted it.

Connie looked at her a bit coldly. "Well, you did ask." Turning to Mary Ellen, she said, "Speaking of traveling, Chuck and I are off to As-pen again soon. I can't wait to escape from this sweltering heat for a few weeks."

"I've heard the weather there is beautiful right now," Dolly said, trying again. "Where are you staying?"

Connie gave Dolly a look that communicated what Southerners meant when they said "Bless your heart," while Mary Ellen told her that Connie and Chuck owned a home in Aspen. Dolly reddened slightly but somehow regained her composure once again. How was she sup-posed to have known that or even guessed it? Obviously, she didn't have much in common with these two women—and possibly not even with Mary Ellen, who seemed nice but whom she didn't really know ei-ther.

"Oh, I beg your pardon," Dolly said to Connie as she wondered why she was apologizing.

"Don't worry. You couldn't have known," she said in a rather condescending tone.

For the next several minutes, Dolly kept silent and listened, chastising herself for assuming she knew what to say to these ladies. Apparently, both led lifestyles very different from hers, and they had money. But their behavior, if not exactly odd, was rather pretentious, like girls in an exclusive college sorority—or members of the *Hark wives* clique.

After the conversation came to a close, Mary Ellen and Dolly went to the bar to grab another glass of wine. Roger and Tim stood alone together on the deck at the other end of the pool, talking about golf. As they chatted, Tim began wondering how soon he and Dolly could politely leave the party. Then Roger abruptly changed the subject.

"Before I forget," Roger said, "and while we have a few minutes alone, I've been meaning to tell you something about our department that you may not know. About once a month, we get together socially with our wives." He smiled and narrowed his eyes. "You know, parties and other events, like meeting for dinner at someone's home and playing cards. If you can't go every time, that's fine, but it's important to participate as much as you can."

"Sounds great." Honestly, Tim thought it sounded like fun. *But important?*

Chapter 9

In late August, the house was finished. After their walk-through, as Dolly and Tim drove to the closing, her thoughts traveled back to the unsolved murder of the teenage girl.

She had decided that Tim was right. Whatever had happened in another house that was long gone had absolutely nothing to do with them and never would. Murders had occurred in other buildings that didn't exist anymore, without any consequences to those who later built on the property. In Europe, there were countless centuries-old structures where people had been tortured and killed long ago, but that didn't keep the buildings from being leased or sold as homes or apartments today. The whole idea that a piece of property could be tainted by a murder and could cause misfortune or sorrow for a future owner now seemed a little crazy to Dolly.

As they walked into the title office that Friday afternoon, her worries vanished, and she was thrilled that they were finally about to turn in the keys to the townhome and get settled in their brand-new home. The movers showed up early the next morning, and she and Tim spent that weekend unpacking and getting organized.

The following day was the first day of school. After Dolly dropped the kids off, she went to the Athletic Club to work out and spent the early afternoon hours unpacking more boxes until it was time to pick up the children. When she turned into the school parking lot, she was surprised to see it filled with parked cars and no semblance of a carpool line. Adults had supervised drop-off that morning, but nobody was manning pickup here. By contrast, in Atlanta, morning and afternoon carpool were organized processes run by a team of teachers who strictly enforced the queue.

There were no buses. Kids either rode in a car or walked home. Dolly meandered her way around the lot, looking for a place to park. Minivans and SUVs sat side by side, engines off and moms behind the wheels. She found a parking space, and at three thirty, the bell rang. Throngs of students streamed out of the building and darted here and there, looking for their ride. But as soon as their own kids got in the car, moms began driving toward the exit.

Dolly was stunned as she watched them go, seemingly not worried about the safety of other people's children. Then Hugh opened the car door and climbed in the passenger seat, and Cole and Audrey hopped in the back.

"Hi, Mom!" Cole said from the back seat as he threw his backpack on the floor.

"Hi. Everybody, put on your seat belts," Dolly said woodenly.

Hugh fastened his seat belt and turned to his mom with a questioning look.

"We'll get going when it's safe," Dolly said, still scanning the chaotic scene. "I can't believe they don't have a carpool line here."

Cole leaned forward. "Isn't it great?"

"I don't think so," she said. Some kid could easily get hit by a car and injured. Or worse.

"When can we go, Mommy?" Audrey whined.

"Not yet."

"Everyone else is leaving," Cole said.

It was true. Most students had found their rides by now, and those who hadn't were gathered on the playground next to the gym to play there unsupervised.

"Why don't they have after-school care?" Dolly asked rhetorically.

The kids' school in Atlanta did. There, after the last car in the long pickup line left, a teacher led the few children who remained over to the gym to join the *regular* after-school care students. If you arrived late to pick up your kids and saw them walking toward the gym, you could drive up and pick them up before they got there, no questions asked. But if you arrived even one second after they were signed in at the gym, you had to pay twenty-five dollars. It was a rigid system, and it worked. This was the opposite, but it looked like parents preferred it this way. Dolly knew that attempting to get it changed would be futile. It was a battle she couldn't win. No one was even going to listen to a newcomer like her propose a different way to do it.

She waited until she didn't see any more kids roaming around and almost all the cars were gone. As she drove away, she resolved to park in the same area and wait until everyone left every day from then on, whether her kids liked it or not. Five minutes later, they were home.

The Garner family settled into the routine of the school year and, with it, homework, sports, and many after-school activities. Audrey was doing fine in class, but her brothers complained that school was a lot harder here—even for Hugh, a straight-A student. Dolly and Tim were aware that the Midwest had a reputation for good schools, and they knew the boys would have work hard to catch up with their classmates.

Heidi's daughter, Ingrid, took dance lessons twice a week, and Audrey wanted to do the same. So Dolly signed her up, and the two girls quickly became friends. Hugh and Cole were baseball players and had just missed the summer Little League season. They wanted to continue as Boy Scouts, so both joined the troop at their school.

Over the next few weeks, Dolly stayed busy organizing the house and hanging pictures and began shopping for living room furniture at the Ethan Allen store on Stockton Road. She was eager to replace their old sofa and chairs, and Tim was happy to let her choose what she wanted and make their new home their own. At the same time, she stayed on top of the never-ending clutter the kids brought home from school every week. She was also the family photographer and kept photo albums chronicling birthdays, holidays, and vacations.

One day in early September, Cole told her he had to do a project for school and went to the basement to start working on it. Before starting dinner that afternoon, she decided to go downstairs to see how he was doing. She found him crafting something three-dimensional that looked more complicated than a typical diorama.

"How's it going?" she asked.

He looked up at her. "Good. I need the superglue, though."

Dolly shuddered. Back when she was in middle school, a classmate got superglue on her fingers while she was doing an art project then touched her eye and got some on her eyeball. While she screamed in pain from the sting, her tears washed out much of it. But some was trapped under her eyelid, and paramedics came and took her to the hospital. Ever since, Dolly had had a phobia of superglue and was afraid to touch a bottle. She couldn't stand to see commercials for it on TV or even walk down a store aisle where it sat on the shelf.

"Dad will be home soon, and I'll ask him to get it for you. But—"

"Where is it? I can get it myself."

"I don't know," she lied. Tim stored it out of her sight on a high shelf in the laundry room. "I think Dad knows. I'll tell him to bring it down when he gets home."

"Okay," Cole said as she hurried back upstairs. "Thanks, Mom."

Twenty minutes later, Tim got home from work. After greeting his wife, he headed upstairs to change clothes.

"Hey," she said to him when he rejoined her in the kitchen where she stood at the counter, chopping tomatoes. "Cole's working on a school project in the basement and needs the superglue. Could you take it down to him and make sure he's careful with it?"

"Sure." He walked up behind her and rested his hands on her shoulders.

She turned and faced him.

"I'll put it back where it goes when he's done," he said.

"Thanks, babe." She let out a deep breath. "Good thing I have you."

Chapter 10

A few weeks later, Tim and Dolly were awakened at three in the morning by the sound of incessant banging. A violent thunderstorm was going on, and the big rectangular crank-out window next to their bed had flown open and was hitting the siding. He jumped out of bed, somehow grasped the edge of the heavy window, and tried to pull it in. Dolly bounded over and crouched near him. Rain slashed at their faces as he played tug-of-war with the window for what felt like several minutes until he was finally able to wedge it into its wooden frame. Dolly ran to get some towels, and he secured the window with them as best as he could.

"How in the world did that happen?" she exclaimed after catching her breath.

He shook his head. "I left it cracked open when we went to bed. Last time I'll ever do that."

Dolly shot him a look. "Good. Don't."

"I'll go get some duct tape. Let's see if we can get it fixed in the morning."

"Mommy? Daddy?" called Audrey from the hall. "What's going on?"

Dolly opened the door. Audrey and Cole were huddled together, their eyes wide. She just fit under his shoulder. Hugh, a heavy sleeper, was apparently still asleep.

"Everything's all right, guys," Dolly said as she reached for them and gave them a hug.

"One of our windows came loose during the storm," said Tim. "It's over now, though. Come on, I'll tuck you both back in bed."

Though it was still raining hard, there was no lightning or thunder anymore, and the wind seemed to have vanished. A few minutes later, Tim rejoined Dolly in the bedroom.

"They're fine," he said, holding the tape. "Are you?"

"I'm okay," she said. "That was pretty wild, though."

He taped the window frame, and they climbed back into bed. "Yeah," he said. "I've never seen anything like it."

She stretched her legs out, trying to relax and go back to sleep. Luckily, she'd been in bed when it happened and hadn't been walking in her sleep. She hadn't done that in a long time, but when she did, Tim didn't always hear her. But if he did, he knew what to do. He didn't startle her, try to wake her, or grab her. He just spoke softly and gently coaxed her back to bed.

⎯⎯◉⎯⎯

The next morning, after Dolly dropped the kids off at school, she tuned in to the local morning news on the radio. According to the report, a straight-line wind, also called a wind shear, had cut a narrow path right through the neighborhood, wreaking havoc in its wake.

"It's somewhat rare, but as you know, it does happen," said the announcer. "We Huntington residents know these straight-line winds can cause a lot of damage within mere moments. We're just lucky it wasn't the precursor to a tornado this time."

She shivered. She had gotten used to the constant wind—it blew almost every day, as Tim had been told. She had never heard of straight-line winds, though.

What else don't I know about Huntington?

As soon as she got home from the Athletic Club, she combed through the yellow pages to look for a handyman. Within minutes, she found one who said he was willing to come over that day to repair the window. Letting a strange man in while she was home alone would be unsettling, but she had no other choice.

He arrived at two o'clock. Gary—the name stitched in bright-blue thread on his tan work shirt—was a heavyset fiftyish white man with a ruddy, weathered face and bad teeth. Dolly introduced herself, and he followed her up to the bedroom and over to the window.

He set down his tool bag next to it. "Looks like you were lucky not to lose it," he said. He paused, turned toward her, and stared. "Those wind shears can be vicious."

"It was pretty unnerving."

"I bet it was." He dropped his eyes and gazed at her chest for a couple seconds before meeting her eyes.

Dolly bristled then shook it off, unwilling to acknowledge the possibility of whatever sordid thoughts he might be having. She crossed her arms in front of her and stood still and silent, vacillating between the idea of watching him work on the window and waiting for him downstairs. Then Gary made her decision for her.

They locked eyes, and he smiled. "The good news is, this won't take long. I'll let you know when I'm done."

She nodded, left the room, and went downstairs.

Twenty minutes later, he walked into the kitchen, where she was sitting in front of the IBM desktop computer, checking email.

"All done," Gary said, smiling. "You'll want to touch up the frame where it got a little banged up, but the window's back to normal. Secure, tight, and functional again."

"Thanks so much. You'll take a check, right?"

"Yes, ma'am," he said, producing an invoice.

Dolly wrote the check, handed it to him, and locked the front door after he left. Then she let out a small sigh of relief, glad to have him out of the house, and watched him drive off.

<hr>

After Tim got home from work, he and Dolly sat down in the living room to have a drink before dinner. The boys were at Scouts, and Audrey was playing up in her room. Heidi's husband, Matt, whose son Noah was in their troop, was giving Cole and Hugh a ride home.

"I told everyone at work about what happened last night," Tim said, "and they were pretty nonchalant about it. Joe said wind shears aren't that uncommon here."

"Well, it was a harrowing way to wake up. It scared the shit out of me. I was afraid you were going to get sucked right out the window."

He rubbed his head. "Honestly, so was I."

"I heard on the radio that wind shears can do serious damage. I didn't see any destruction around town today, though."

"Roger told me they strike low to the ground and that they're very narrow and direct—hence the term straight-line. So the damage they do cause isn't really widespread."

"Thank God. Even though this one managed to hit *our* house."

Chapter 11

One day at the Athletic Club, Dolly and Heidi chatted on the way to the locker room.

"So, have you started feeling like five miles is a long way to drive yet?" Heidi asked.

"I have," Dolly admitted. "But everywhere I go is closer than that. It does feel weird."

"Well, you can drive all the way across town in twenty minutes. I call it small-town creep," Heidi said, smiling. "And the way people drive here too! Like grandmas and grandpas."

Dolly laughed. "If I dare to pull out into an intersection and make a left turn on a yellow light—"

"You probably get the evil eye."

Dolly nodded. "Yep. Feels that way anyway."

"Don't you know by now that you're supposed to sit where you are, cycle through the light, and wait for a green arrow?" Heidi smirked.

"And you better not go over the speed limit," Dolly added.

They laughed, and then Heidi added, "What do you say we go out to lunch soon? We need to celebrate our birthdays." Hers was the following week, and Dolly's was a few days later.

"Great idea," she said.

They decided to meet the next Friday at Ardennes Country Club, where Matt and Heidi were also members. It was located in Elmwood, a small community just east of the city limits. Besides an eighteen-hole golf course, the club boasted eight tennis courts, an Olympic-size outdoor pool, a restaurant, and an inn called the Lodge which offered a dozen guest rooms. It was a very nice club, but it wasn't the poshest or the most exclusive one in town. The ritziest club, reserved for the elite upper crust, was called Huntington Country Club. Dolly had learned that its members included Peter Hark and several high-level Hark executives.

Dolly walked into the restaurant at Ardennes and saw Heidi waiting at a table for two.

"Sorry I'm late," she said.

"No worries. I just got here."

They began talking about kids and husbands, and after they ordered, Heidi mentioned that a few other wives of Hark executives she knew or was acquainted with were seated nearby. Most were married to men who worked in the shipping department with Matt or to other transportation colleagues.

"I wouldn't call any of them Stepford Wives," Heidi said in a low tone. "Many of them are transplants like us and pretty down to earth. Most have school-age kids too. Some are stay-at-home moms, and some are career moms."

"Hark wives who work outside the home?" Dolly asked, feigning shock.

Heidi grinned. "If they work, they do it because they *want* to, not because they have to. I know two who are accountants and another who's an attorney." She cocked her head.

"Real career women," Dolly said. "I can't imagine juggling a career and motherhood right now."

"Oh, they have help," Heidi said, her eyes wide. "A *lot* of help. You can bet on that."

They both knew that many career women relished the power that earning high incomes afforded them and that almost all of them had nannies, maids, gardeners, and even cooks.

"I'm sure they do," Dolly said. "I don't wish I had a big career, but I've thought about getting a part-time job when the kids get a little older. If I can find one, that is."

"Not me, girl." Heidi shook her head. "I don't think I could handle the stress of balancing even a part-time job with raising three kids. Even when they're teenagers. *Especially* when they're teenagers. Since Matt makes plenty of money, I don't think I'll have to." She shrugged.

Dolly felt the same way—for now. Hugh was a teen already, and Cole would be one soon. And when Audrey was that age, she didn't want her to be home alone after school if she didn't have to be. However, she and Tim would see how things were going when the time came, and if she need to contribute to their income, she would find a way. But it could be very difficult for her to find something after opting out of the corporate world for so long—unless she went back to school first. During the time Tim had been with Hark, they had rebuilt their savings almost to what it was a few years ago, and they were back on their feet financially. College for three kids was going to cost a lot, though.

"I'm sure the teenage years will be challenging," Dolly said. "With Hugh, so far so good. But who knows?"

"Speaking of kids," Heidi said, "what are y'all are doing for Thanksgiving? Are you going to Atlanta?"

Dolly shook her head. "Mom and her husband live in Florida, and they spend it with her son and his family. Tim's got a brother up north, and my sister lives in California, but both do their own thing, and so do we."

"You aren't close to your sister?" Heidi paused for a second. "Forgive me for being so direct. You know how I am. I don't mean to pry, though."

"No, it's fine," Dolly said, "and being direct is good—I like people who say what they mean." She smiled. "Plus, I don't mind telling you. My sister and I aren't close. She's six years older and is single with no kids. We talk once a while but not often."

"I have a brother like that," Heidi said. "We've never been close. He's a couple years older and lives in Chicago, and I hear from him once in a while but haven't seen him in years. We're going down to Houston for Thanksgiving to see Matt's parents."

Once again, Dolly was grateful to have someone in town she could relate to. Knowing that she and Heidi had so much in common made Dolly feel closer to her new friend.

That afternoon, Dolly stopped off at the cleaners and the video store then went to pick up the kids. After school, all three played outside before doing their homework. Few people in the neighborhood had fences, and backyards flowed into one another, creating a large meadow. Dolly kept an eye out for her children when they played outside through the kitchen window. The boys were under orders to keep Audrey with them at all times, and as far as Dolly knew, they obeyed.

———◦———

A couple weeks later, Tim and Dolly met Heidi and Matt for dinner on Saturday night at Mia's, a brand-new restaurant on Stockton Road, the town's busiest avenue, lined with fast food restaurants, gas stations, and strip shopping centers. The next morning, Dolly went downstairs to make coffee while Tim walked out to the driveway to pick up the newspaper. Hugh, Cole, and Audrey were still asleep upstairs.

Tim came into the kitchen and thrust the paper in front of Dolly. Her eyes fell to the front-page headline.

East Side Home Invasion
Three Dead, One Survivor

Chapter 12

Tim leaned over Dolly's shoulder as they read the article in the Sunday paper.

According to the report, none of the victims had been identified yet. The lone survivor, a kindergarten teacher, had told police that late the night before, three men broke into the rental house she shared with her fiancé. Another couple had joined them there for dinner. The men held them at gunpoint, raped the women, and then loaded them all into a commercial van. They drove around town to ATMs and had each victim withdraw as much cash as possible. Then they took them to a deserted field on the outskirts of town, lined them up, and shot each one of them in the head.

Tim's pulse raced as he read on. *How in the world could something like this happen here in Huntington?* The article said the teacher survived because the bullet was somehow deflected by her barrette and only grazed her head. She played dead until the men drove away, and then she ran through the snow to the nearest house with its lights on and banged on the door. The occupants let her in and wrapped her in a blanket. She told them what had happened, and they called the police.

Dolly looked up from the paper and at Tim. Her face was white. "Oh my God. This happened two miles from here."

Tim felt as if he'd been sucker punched in the gut. He sat down beside her. "At least they already got the killers. With her as a witness, they can nail them."

She closed her eyes. "We can't let the boys see this."

"They never look at the paper. Except for the sports page."

"Then let's only give them that," Dolly said.

They would find out, though. Hugh would anyway. Huntington was a small town. Chances were he had a friend who was connected in some way to one of the victims. Whenever and however he heard what had happened, it would certainly shake him up. Tim wanted to shield him, his siblings, and their mother from everything that was evil and horrific. Knowing that he couldn't do so made him feel powerless—and hollow inside.

❦

The next day, Joe called Tim into his office. Joe's face was pale, and his eyes were glassy.

"You saw the news," he said. Tim nodded. "Everyone around here is pretty shaken up. One of the victims was Jake Miller."

Tim's hand flew to his mouth. "Roger's assistant? Oh no. That's awful."

"Yeah. He's the one engaged to the girl who survived. It was his house they broke into."

Tim shook his head. "God, he's so young. What is he, twenty-four?"

"He was twenty-three. Roger is here at the office, but he's pretty somber, as you might imagine. So is everybody. My secretary is going to find out about the arrangements and will let people know." Joe's eyes met Tim's. "I hope those monsters get the death penalty."

Tim closed his eyes for a second and let out a deep breath. "Thanks for letting me know, Joe."

That evening when he got home from work, Tim told Dolly about Jake. Then they went up to their bedroom and turned on the six o'clock news while he changed clothes. The Huntington police were holding a live news conference and revealed the victims' names to the public. All had known each other since they were teenagers. The kindergarten teacher, Jake's fiancée, worked at the school that Heidi and Matt's children attended. The police chief announced that they had arrested three suspects.

A reporter asked, "Do you have any reason to believe that any of them could be the serial killer who's been terrorizing our community for over two decades and is still at large?"

Tim walked over to the bed and sat down beside Dolly. "What serial killer?" he murmured.

"No, we don't," said the chief, his face stony. "We believe that the serial killer you're referring to, known as the Barbie Killer, is middle-aged or older. These men are much younger. And the Barbie Killer always acts alone."

"Do you believe that the Barbie Killer is still in Huntington, then, and is lurking around somewhere out there in our community?"

The chief cleared his throat. "No comment. No more questions at this time. Thank you."

Chapter 13

He was furious.

The town had erupted in fear of him again but not because of anything he had done lately. Those degenerates shocked everyone—including him—by what they did to the four young people. But those idiots screwed up and botched things, and they had already been arrested.

How do you shoot someone in the head and miss? he wondered. *How, and why, do you not make sure they're all dead before you take off?*

He had made a grave error only once, and he had learned from it. Luckily, it hadn't led anyone to him, but he'd been afraid that it would for a long time. When he made his blunder, he'd been stone-cold sober, of course, but these fools had probably been hammered on alcohol or high on drugs. They were amateurs out looking for fun, and their one big mistake was going to cost them their lives.

Because Kansas had the death penalty.

It was gratifying to hear the press and the police chief call him by his nickname, though. People hadn't forgotten about him, even after all this time. He hadn't killed anyone in seven years. He'd been too busy. He had responsibilities, he had a wife and children, and he had his hobbies. He was leading what people called a normal life, and weeks turned into months and months into years. Others treated him with respect, and no one suspected him. But maybe the reason it had been so long was because the demons had been sleeping all this time. If so, this unexpected and new development might awaken them.

In any case, he wanted to know more about the crime. He would never have done it that way, so that reporter was an imbecile. He would have killed the men right away, and then he would have done what he wished to the women. That was only logical. Get the threats out of the way first—or try to. There was no reason to make them watch, for God's sake. And under no circumstances would he ever have done it with two other men. He would never take that kind of risk. It was needless and stupid. And as the chief said, he always acted alone.

He stalked his victims and looked for opportunity. In a way, it was up to chance. To gain entrance to their homes was so easy, it was almost ridiculous. All he had to do was knock on the door, say his car had broken down, and ask to use the telephone. Sometimes, he only had to ask for a glass of water on a hot day. As long as he was well-dressed, that usually worked. Of course, he gave them a fake name.

He was choosy about his victims. That was why years had passed since his last mission was completed. That was what he called them—missions. When they were finished, the demons would rest for a while, and he could live his life as before.

He knew he was leading a double life, but what choice did he have? And because people were talking about him again, the demons would take note of it and might force him to act. He could put them off for a little while, but in the end, he knew he would have to satisfy them. If he didn't, his urges would persist, his "need," as he called it, would go unmet, and he would feel no relief until he did their bidding.

Chapter 14

That televised news conference was the way Tim and Dolly found out about the Barbie Killer, the murderer who had been hiding in plain sight in Huntington since the 1970s.

Dolly was shocked by his existence and astonished when the reporter said he had "been terrorizing our community for over two decades and is still at large." When the police chief refused to confirm whether he was still in the community, it had to mean that he believed the killer was indeed "lurking around" and looking for his next victim.

No wonder everybody at the book club meeting that night had been amazed when Celeste announced she felt safe and never worried about crime. It was almost as if she had chosen to be in denial about something that everyone else knew about but didn't bring up because they didn't want to reveal the town secret. Only Betsy and Susie had spoken up about their concerns about crime. The fact that no one dared to mention the Barbie Killer was extremely odd. Dolly thought of all of them—except Heidi—as her *non-Hark girlfriends*, for lack of a better term, and up until now, she'd thought of them all as honest, down-to-earth, and friendly.

Maybe they'd hidden the truth from her because she hadn't lived here long and they didn't want to scare her—and because the killer hadn't been active in a long time. She considered calling Betsy and asking her everything she knew about him—and why nobody had told her about him—but she didn't want to sound accusatory and possibly alienate her. So she decided to find out everything she could on her own about the Barbie Killer and his victims. While she was at it, she would do what she should have done months earlier and research the murder committed on her property back in the sixties. There had to be some information about it somewhere, and if nothing else, it would make her feel better to know more.

———◆———

The next day, she went back to the library and combed through the archives of *The Huntington Post,* searching for articles about murders in Huntington during the 1960s. As she skimmed through microfiche, she counted ten, and from what she could tell, only one of them, committed in 1964, remained unsolved. *Bingo.*

Denise Hutchins was the victim's name. As Betsy said, her throat had been slashed. She bled to death in her bedroom while her parents slept, and there was no sign of a break-in or forced entry to the home. Evidently, Denise let the perpetrator in that night, so police believed the killer was someone she knew. Her boyfriend, Randy Hoffman, was the prime suspect, but the police weren't able to locate him. They searched for months without success, the murder weapon was never found, and DNA profiling hadn't been done at the time. Having hit a dead end, Dolly felt defeated yet glad she tried. Next, she searched through the archives for articles about the Barbie Killer. Over the next few hours, she was able to piece together his history of killing and learned how he got his nickname.

His first victim was a single woman in her twenties. He killed her in the early 1970s in her home in the West Side. After cutting the phone line outside, he broke in through a window, waited for her, overpowered her, and tied her to a bed before strangling her to death. Police found a Polaroid photograph of a naked Barbie doll next to the body, its hair color the same as the victim's.

Imagining the murder scene made Dolly shiver. The killer had done some planning and had brought what he needed with him. Why a Barbie doll, and what did it mean? And why would any man do this? She kept searching for information and was horrified by what she read.

Over the next three years, he'd murdered four more young women the same way, making him a serial killer. Each time, he left a Polaroid of a Barbie doll that resembled the victim next to the body, but he was careful not to leave any fingerprints, shoe prints, or any other incriminating evidence. Nor did he leave the actual doll. Huntington police had begun strongly suggesting that all women make sure that their phone lines were uncut before they entered their homes.

Dolly felt sick. Picking up the phone and finding the line dead would be frightening, and hearing—or seeing—an intruder in your house would be terrifying, She wiped the perspiration from her brow and tried to unclench her teeth. *Take a breath and finish this.*

During the next six years, she learned, no murders had occurred. The townspeople must have relaxed a bit but were probably bracing themselves for the next one. Then one day, the Barbie Killer had struck again. This time he broke into his twenty-something victim's home, apparently unaware that her boyfriend was there. The Barbie Killer stabbed him with a kitchen knife and left him for dead. Then he tied up the woman, beat and tortured her, and strangled her. The boyfriend, who had passed out, somehow survived but was unable to identify the killer. All he remembered was that he was a white man of average height with brown hair and looked "ordinary." Over the next several months, police picked up and questioned over a thousand men who fit that general description, but finding no leads, they had eventually given up.

The terror this community had been through was astounding. Dolly's stomach was in knots as she thought about what it must have been like.

Then she read that in the mid-1980s, two more women, both in their early thirties, had gone missing. Their bodies were found months later in ditches on the edge of town, along with weather-beaten Polaroids of a Barbie doll. Both had their ankles and wrists bound with twine and had been stabbed several times and strangled. A few weeks after the second one was discovered, the newspaper editor received handwritten messages signed *The Barbie Killer* claiming responsibility for both of the murders. Sales of residential security systems had skyrocketed.

Dolly took a deep breath. *Thank God we have one.*

According to the reports she read, the killer had strangled his victims with a rope, a belt, pantyhose, or his hands. Most were found with a plastic grocery store bag tied over their heads. As Dolly and Tim had learned while watching the news conference, the last homicide took place in 1988, just seven years ago. That time, the victim was a thirty-year-old married woman with two children. One day, while one kid was at school and the other, a toddler, was taking a nap, the Barbie Killer broke in through a window. A few hours later, the husband came home from work early to pack for a business trip. He found his wife's dead body and a photo of a Barbie on the floor in the bedroom. Their two-year-old son had still been in his crib.

That family had lived half a mile away from the Garners.

Chapter 15

Dolly told Tim everything she had learned about the serial killer, and he was as creeped out as she was about the location of his last murder.

Over the next few days, though, no mention was made in the media or at Tim's office about the Barbie Killer. Because Jake was one of the home invasion victims, he and the crime were all that anyone talked about. The funeral was that Friday at St. Mark's Episcopal Church, and along with several of Tim's co-workers, Tim and Dolly were going.

Tim couldn't stop thinking about the horrific crime or what Jake had endured. The randomness and brutality of it reminded him of *In Cold Blood* by Truman Capote, the true story of a family murdered in their beds in Kansas.

The home invasion murders had made the national news, and despite the effort Tim and Dolly made to hide it from the boys, they found out. Tim wondered if Audrey had heard about it as well. She hadn't said anything, so they didn't mention it, but if she brought it up, they had agreed they would tell her about it in simple but honest terms. The boys said they'd heard people discussing it and describing what the victims went through.

Tim and Dolly decided to sit down with them and let Tim do most of the talking. He wasn't sure if they knew about the Barbie Killer, but if so, he was ready to talk about that as well.

"Some people are evil," he said to the boys, point blank. "That's just the way it is. The men who did this are, and they'll be punished for it. The police already have them in custody."

Cole's blue eyes were watery. "Why did they do it, Dad?" he asked softly.

Dolly reached for Cole's arm, and Tim shook his head. "Nobody really knows, son." Then he looked at Hugh, who wore a stoic expression yet seemed clearly troubled. "It was a very cruel and savage act. It was barbaric. But they're in jail now, and they're not getting out."

Dolly sat beside her husband on the sofa, her hands clasped in front of her. "Dad's right. It's over, and they can't hurt anyone else."

They continued discussing it for a few more minutes, and neither of the boys brought up the serial killer.

Later that evening, when all three kids were in the basement, watching television, and Dolly and Tim were in the kitchen finishing up, she rinsed the last plate, put it in the dishwasher, and turned toward him. "Tim, is there any way you can get transferred back to Atlanta?"

They had danced around the subject once or twice before but had never addressed it.

"You know the answer, babe. No. At least, not right now."

"Why don't you look for another job somewhere else, then? We could move again. Anywhere." She leaned back against the counter, a tired look on her face.

"If I had been with Hark longer, I would, and I think I'd be able to find one. But I've only been with them for a year now. To any potential employer, I'd look like a job-hopper or, worse, like I'm about to get fired. I don't know how I could keep them from thinking one or the other."

"Maybe you could just explain what's going on and be honest about why you want to change jobs. Say that things are fine at Hark but that you want to leave Huntington."

Tim pressed his lips together. "I really don't think that would fly, babe. Besides, crime is everywhere. You know that. Murders happen in all cities, big and small."

"But we thought this was a safe place to live, Tim. A great place to raise a family."

"I know, doll. But what if I get a job somewhere else and we move there, and then we find out about murders happening there too? Or about another serial killer?"

Dolly shut her eyes for a second. "Honestly, I'm almost more upset that no one at Hark ever told us about him before we got here than I am about him being out there."

Tim raised his arms to his sides, palms up, starting to feel exasperated. "What were they going to say? 'Move to Huntington, but be advised there's a serial killer who's been on the loose here for over twenty years'?"

Dolly spoke slowly. "Yes, that's exactly what they should have told us."

"Dolly, I know you didn't want to move here, but—"

"Hark has a motive to keep it a secret," she said. "If they didn't do that, it'd be even harder for them to get qualified people to move to company headquarters. To 'attract talent,' in the words of your boss."

Talent they presume will buy into Hark culture, in and out of the office—especially if they pay them enough.

"We don't know that."

Dolly rolled her eyes. "Aren't *you* upset that nobody told us about the Barbie Killer?"

He ran a hand through his hair and looked her in the eye. "No, not particularly. Why should they have? I mean, I don't like it, but the last murder he committed was back in the 80s."

"And it happened a half mile away!" Dolly knew he could be stubborn, but she wasn't going to let up. "No matter what you say, I would rather have known about him before we got here, and I can't believe you don't feel the same way."

"I do feel the same way. But we can't change what happened here, and we can't make things be different from the way they are. We can't fix it, either by moving away or by staying here. We just built a big, beautiful new home that we love. We've gotten settled and made some new friends. I thought you were adjusting and even starting to like it here."

"I was, and I am. But I'm scared, Tim."

"I know, babe. We can't live in fear, though."

She looked up at the ceiling and then back at her husband. Yes, she *could* live in fear. She already was. "Maybe I should make sure the phone line hasn't been cut each time I get home."

He scratched his chin. "That's a good idea. But don't go around to the back to check. Just pick up the phone as soon as you walk in the door and make sure you hear a dial tone."

"What if I don't?"

He shuddered. "Then get out of the house. Fast."

⎯⎯◉⎯⎯

That night as he lay in bed, trying to sleep, Tim's mind drifted back to his discussion with Dolly. He didn't know why he'd been reluctant to admit it to her, but the truth was that he *was* angry that nobody had mentioned the killer to him before he moved his family to Huntington. If they had, at least he wouldn't have done so believing that it was a safe place to live. And he might have even refused to move or started looking for another job elsewhere.

Tomorrow, he would bring it up and tell her just that and say he was sorry that he hadn't said so. Maybe no one at Hark had set out to deceive him. But they, and the people who lived in this town, had lied to him by omission, which was just as bad. It was as if the town's motto was "What you don't know won't hurt you."

Huntington clearly wasn't the safe, family-oriented town he had been led to believe it was. Even though criminals were everywhere, serial killers—and ruthless murderers—weren't. Knowing that a serial killer was lurking around and had eluded police for decades frightened Tim, and it unnerved him. He couldn't sit back and wait. He had to protect his family.

He had to buy a gun, and he and Dolly needed to learn to use it.

She had always been totally against having a weapon in the house. So far, he hadn't pushed it because he didn't see the need. But he wasn't convinced that a residential security system was enough to prevent a break-in—or worse. Having a gun in the house made all kinds of sense, and he thought it would give both of them peace of mind.

He would talk to her about it and convince her it was a good idea. He needed to think of a good place to store it too—somewhere the kids wouldn't happen to find it.

He closed his eyes and tried to get some sleep. Although he still thought Dolly's suggestion that their property was cursed was irrational, he certainly hoped that she was wrong.

Chapter 16

Dolly did exactly what Tim suggested and began checking the phone for a dial tone every time she came home. The first few times, she was afraid of what might happen if the line was dead.

Can I get out of the house fast enough?

After about two weeks, though, her anxiety started to fade a little. She checked the line every time, but she reasoned that the Barbie Killer wasn't stupid. He knew that long ago, the police had advised women to check their phone lines, so he probably wasn't cutting them anymore. Maybe he wasn't even breaking into houses because of it. If he were still active, maybe he was attacking women elsewhere.

However, her shock and astonishment about his existence and the nature of his crimes hadn't waned. How could a plain vanilla town like Huntington be terrorized for over two decades by a murderer who had never been found? Had the police given up on finding him for good? And if so, why? If not—and she couldn't imagine that they had given up—maybe they'd asked the press not to report much about him as part of a strategy not to feed his ego and possibly stir him up. Either way, since the last murder had been seven years ago, there'd been no reason to report on him.

Dolly's resolve to fit in and to adapt to life in Huntington began to weaken too. How could she trust anyone now, other than those few people she'd met who weren't from this town? She had been blindsided when she found out about the killer. Heidi had been unaware of the Barbie Killer as well and had also been shocked. And now that the secret was out, Dolly thought people were acting more suspicious of others than usual. Maybe the Midwestern trait of keeping to yourself was a natural, intelligent reaction to the fact that a killer was in their midst.

Don't look at anybody, and you may stay safe.

She tried not to think about it, and at times, she was success-ful—but it was always in the back of her mind. She kept herself oc-cupied, and her routine stayed the same. She got up, fed the children, and took them to school. She spent her days working out, cleaning the house, shopping, and running errands. Housewife stuff. After school, it was time for homework, activities, and dinner. Mom stuff.

Christmas was just around the corner, and that meant decorating the house, sending cards, and wrapping presents. The busier she stayed getting ready for the holidays, the more she could numb herself, calm her nerves, and allay her fears. On the 26th, she and Tim took the kids to Disney World for a week, a treat that both were pleased they could easily afford now. They got home on the first of January, and school started a few days later. Once the holidays were over, Dolly almost for-got to be afraid.

And then, at the end of January, a forty-year-old woman who lived in the East Side went missing.

<hr>

Her name was Barbara Isom—Barb, to her friends—the woman Dolly had accidentally eavesdropped on at the Athletic Club that time back in August, who'd said to her friend Shelly that she had "nothing but hate in her heart" for "that man."

What if Barbara Isom's body turned up, and the Barbie Killer had murdered her? She'd be his first victim who could be called Barbie, which was downright creepy, and Dolly was already spooked because of her own name. His last two victims had gone missing months before their bodies had been discovered. But police—and the local press—centered on Barb's husband.

Martin Isom was an engineer with Boeing. According to Heidi, who got it from Celeste, several months earlier his wife had found out that he was having an affair. He told her he had ended it, and they started seeing a marriage counselor. However, a few days before she disappeared, Barb had filed for divorce.

Martin hadn't been arrested—there was no body yet—but because he was the husband, he was the police department's number one suspect. He told them he'd thought his wife had forgiven him and that he was shocked when he learned she was leaving him. He claimed he was out of his mind with worry about her, he was afraid she'd been murdered, and that they were wasting their time grilling him rather than looking for her. Over the next couple of days, there was still no sign of her, nor had Martin received any messages from her.

If she was dead, Dolly hoped that he had killed her.

Days passed. She didn't turn up, and people kept whispering about her disappearance and Martin.

———◉———

Susie hosted the next book club meeting. Dolly had attended almost every month, and she went to this one even though she had only just started the book. Heidi, Celeste, and many of the regulars showed up that night too. Lots of them belonged to the Athletic Club and knew Barb or were acquainted with her. Celeste and her husband, Bob, were friends with Barb and Martin.

"They go to our church," she told everyone that evening.

"Have you seen Martin lately?" asked Betsy.

Celeste nodded. "He's a total mess." She sighed.

"You don't think he killed her, do you?" Susie asked, her eyes wide.

Celeste shrugged. "No, I don't. But who knows? I mean, you think you know people, but... like they say, you never know what goes on behind closed doors. Frankly, I was shocked when I heard she wanted a divorce."

In their social circle and on their side of town, especially with so many Hark families living there, divorce certainly wasn't unheard of—although it was rare, even if infidelity might not be. Like Dolly and

Tim, most couples their age had been married for a while. But whether they were happily married or not was another story.

However, most of the wives had a strong incentive to make their marriages work and to make them a priority. Because their husbands were very good providers, they lived affluent lifestyles and didn't have to worry about money. They wanted their children to grow up in an intact, nuclear family, and when they felt distant from their husbands, they didn't give up on their marriages or look for affection elsewhere. So the idea that a man would cheat on his wife and then turn around and murder her was very hard to wrap their heads around—even if the wife wanted a divorce and had been unfaithful as well.

"Well, I choose to believe Martin," said Heidi. "Unless and until there's a reason not to."

"You mean, until they find her body," Celeste said.

"If they do, that doesn't mean that *he* killed her," Dolly put in. "The Barbie Killer could have done it."

There, she'd said it. But everyone looked at her as if she had just proposed they all run down the street naked.

Susie broke the silence. "Maybe he did do it, and *he's* the Barbie Killer."

Heidi drew in a sharp breath as Celeste whirled around.

"What? That's crazy," Celeste blurted out.

Susie studied the floor, as if she'd been chastised.

Celeste turned to Dolly. "Honestly, no one really talks about the Barbie Killer anymore. At least, *I* don't."

"How is that crazy? And why don't they talk about him?" Heidi asked.

Because even though the secret's out about him, that's taboo? Why?

Celeste shook her head. "Because it's ancient history, and he's got to be dead by now. Even if he's still alive and he lives here, he's way too old to be out there killing anyone. Or he could already be in prison for another crime."

"Well, I for one hope he's dead," said Betsy, shaking her head.

Dolly silently agreed, and she was more than a little astonished by Celeste's pronouncements. The Barbie Killer *might* be dead, but if he wasn't, why was Celeste so sure that he was too old to kill again? And the idea that he was in prison was hard to believe since the police hadn't stopped hunting him. Celeste could brush aside the danger they were all in if she wanted to, but Dolly wasn't going to rest well at night until the Barbie Killer was captured and in prison. People could relax and pretend that he wasn't out there, but she couldn't do either.

And she certainly wasn't going to take it lying down or put on blinders and act like all was well.

What kind of a place harbors a serial killer that everyone's afraid to mention?

Why are people so close to the vest, not just about themselves but about Huntington's history of murder? What kind of town is this, and what else don't I know?

⸻⊙⸻

When book club was over, Heidi and Dolly left together and got into Heidi's car. Although neither lived far from Susie's house, they didn't want to walk home in the dark, and Heidi had volunteered to drive.

"What the hell is with Celeste?" Heidi exclaimed as soon as they shut their car doors. "Why is she so convinced that the Barbie Killer isn't out there anymore, about to kill again?"

"And why did she jump on Susie like that? Barb's husband *might* have killed her."

Heidi started the car. "*And* he might be the Barbie Killer. It's not impossible."

"I read that two of his victims were missing for months before they were found, lying in ditches," Dolly said. "All the others were discovered in their homes."

"My God," Heidi said. "I hope Barb turns up soon, whether she's dead or alive."

Whatever had happened to her, Dolly felt sure that the killer was alive and nearby and that it was only a matter of time before his next murder.

Any white man aged forty or older could be the Barbie Killer. He could be the landlord of the townhome they had rented last summer—she had never met him, but Tim had—who'd left their door unlocked and the keys in the kitchen for them. He could be Gary, the guy who'd fixed the window after the wind shear hit their house. He could be the owner of the video store, the produce manager at Dillons, or a loan officer at the bank. He might be a parishioner at their church, one of their neighbors, or even one of Tim's co-workers.

He could even be married to someone that Dolly knew.

Chapter 17

His wife sat down across from him at the kitchen table on Saturday morning.

"That poor man," she said as she perused the front page of the newspaper, where a story about the missing woman appeared at the top.

"You don't think he killed her?" he asked.

She looked up, and they locked eyes for a moment. "I don't want to believe it. Do you?"

"I don't know. He might have." He picked up the sports page.

She shook her head. "That's true. Isn't it always the husband?"

He shrugged and sipped his coffee. "Men are pigs, and some of them are monsters."

She got up and poured herself another cup. "Well, if he's innocent, I feel sorry for him. He must be terribly worried, waiting to hear from her."

"Not if he's guilty. Sounds like he had motive too."

"If she's dead, it could have been someone else," she said. "It may have been random, like those young people who were murdered back in December."

"Hmm," he said.

"Or it could be the Barbie Killer, come out from wherever he's been hiding all these years. If he's still alive."

"I doubt that," he said. "But in any case, don't worry about him. You're safe with me."

"If you say so, honey," she said as she refilled his coffee cup.

That afternoon he drove past the Glenlake subdivision, just a few miles from his home. The last house built in it was owned by a family who had moved here from Georgia. The two boys often played outside and roamed around the neighborhood. Sometimes their little sister would tag along, but they usually ditched her. Then she would wander around alone.

He had been about the size of that little girl when the lying began. He didn't know when he'd told his first lie, but in the beginning he only told harmless fibs and half-truths. Little white lies. Everyone did that, so why shouldn't he? He did it mainly to avoid punishment anyway. His father didn't believe in sparing the rod—or the whip. His mother was of the same mind. He spent his youth in fear of both and trying not to upset either one. And after he started lying, he couldn't stop. He felt bad about it at first, but then he got used to it and soon turned into a compulsive liar. And lying was just like acting anyway. It was only make-believe.

At some point, reality and make-believe got twisted up in his mind, though, and he started telling downright lies and stories—not only to avoid getting in trouble but merely because he could. Just to see how far he could go, to test what he could make others believe. That was the acting part, the storytelling part. At times, it bothered him, as if he had a conscience. But that disappeared. Before he knew it, lying was a habit that he was unable to shake, like sneaking around and spying on people, and eventually, stalking some of them.

He had never told his wife about any of that or much at all about his childhood. He'd never told her that he wet the bed until he was twelve and that his father beat him mercilessly for it. He'd never mentioned how isolated he felt when he was growing up or how lost. How he spent so much time daydreaming in the woods, wanting to get away from the turmoil and tension at home. He knew he would get out of there one day, but he often felt like that day would never come. He spent hours alone, fantasizing about growing up to be an assassin who lived in the shadows. He didn't know how to square that with the need to earn a living, though. There was no one to turn to then, so he learned to keep to himself. His only choice was to be adaptable. He learned to be self-reliant and sneaky because he had no other choice.

When he was a teenager, he started catching animals and torturing them. That was a red flag, he knew—if anyone found out, he would have been in deep trouble. But he did it all the same, just to see what a living thing could survive and what he was capable of doing to it. He was fascinated with setting fires, too, and sometimes he burned the animals alive. When he did that, he felt like he could be someone else, a different person from the one he was expected to be. Eventually, he channeled that feeling into becoming a chameleon, and he got quite good at it. He would do or say whatever it took to be accepted, to talk his way into a situation, and to pretend that he was someone that he wasn't.

Then one day he broke into someone's house for the first time. He chose that house because the sliding glass door to the kitchen was easy to jimmy and they didn't have any pets. He watched and waited until he knew the family was gone for the day. When he got inside, he took his time and looked in all the drawers and closets. He even looked under the beds. He didn't find anything interesting or worth taking, but he moved the living room furniture around just to mess with them.

After that, there was no turning back. He was hooked. Sneaking into and searching other peoples' homes for valuable items became his favorite hobby, and he started taking what he wanted. He stole cash, jewelry, ladies' underwear, and even letters. Later, he began taking knives, small tools, and anything else potentially useful that he could fit in his pockets. He stored his treasures in a long wooden box that he stashed underneath his twin bed.

It was about that time when he heard the demons speak to him for the first time, and they soon forced themselves on him. Up until then, he'd had the strength to keep them away. He also began reading crime novels and detective magazines, studying criminals' methods and police procedures, and taking copious notes about both. He kept his notes in his box as well. Then, one day, not long after his time in the service, his strength vanished, and the demons pushed him to do the things he did. Before long, he started idolizing notorious murderers that he had read about, and an enormous fantasy world built around violence and sadism took root inside his head.

He knew that he was different from other people, but he couldn't help it. He was who he was, and he couldn't change. Nor did he want to. Over the years, with each beating and with each blow, little by little, any feelings of empathy he'd ever had for others had drained away. Eventually, after years of abuse, he had become the abuser. He directed it at his missions, according to the demons' will, and he had no choice other than to satisfy his urges.

He still had his wooden box, but now he stored it with his tools out in his shed, next to his workbench. He kept the box locked, of course. When he completed a mission, he always took a few souvenirs—a drivers' license or other ID, or a photo or two. He kept a journal in there, too, where he recorded how his missions went down, how he killed his victims, the positions he left them in, and what errors he made—they were few. He also kept his collection of Barbie dolls in the box. All were naked. Some were blondes, and some were brunettes. He had thoughtfully chosen each of them, and in some cases, he had cut their hair to resemble his missions.

He was a careful man, very detail oriented, and self-doubt wasn't in his nature. And he was proud of how far he had come in life and everything he had accomplished, especially considering his turbulent childhood. If for some reason he failed to complete a mission—if he had to abandon it—that was unfortunate, but it was okay. He would move on, and the next time he would try it another way, maybe after doing a practice run on a similar one. It was all part of the game.

Chapter 18

Almost a week after her disappearance, Barbara Isom resurfaced. Just like that.

Police told the media she had reconnected with an old college roommate, and they'd decided to meet in Las Vegas for a girls' weekend. Three nights had turned into six, and because she and Martin were barely speaking when she left, she didn't bother to contact him or let him know where she was. When she came home, she was amazed that he'd reported her missing.

The town heaved a sigh of relief, and everyone stopped whispering and went back to normal. Everyone except Dolly.

On Friday, Dolly met Heidi at noon at Ardennes. Having lunch at the club together had become a monthly habit, and Dolly was looking forward to seeing her friend. When she walked into the lobby, she saw her standing in the center of it, speaking to a woman whose back was turned. Dolly walked toward them, and when the woman whirled around to face her, Dolly's jaw dropped.

She felt like she was looking in the mirror.

"See what I mean?" Heidi said to the woman. "Dolly Garner, meet Maggie Burns, your doppelgänger! I walked up to her and thought she was you!"

This was just like Heidi, thought Dolly. Rather than murmuring something like "Excuse me—I thought you were someone else," she'd started talking to the woman. But Heidi could talk to anybody, and most people were attracted to her charm and confidence.

"I apologize for startling you," Heidi said to Maggie. "I really thought you were Dolly." Heidi looked at her friend with a twinkle in her eye. "You sure you don't have a twin sister you've never mentioned?"

Dolly smiled and shook her head. She gazed at Maggie's face, looking for differences. Her eyes were brown as well, but they were a bit darker. Her lips were shaped like Dolly's but not as full—and her lipstick was a different shade. They *did* look a lot alike but not identical.

"They say everybody has a double," Dolly said. She'd always thought a friend of hers and Tim's in Atlanta was a dead ringer for a young Bill Clinton and that Tim's last boss looked just like San Francisco 49ers quarterback Joe Montana.

Maggie cocked her head. "I guess this proves it. Who knows? Maybe we're distantly related." Even Maggie's voice—and her accent—were like Dolly's.

"I don't mean to be nosy, but you don't sound like a Midwesterner," Dolly said.

"Oh, you're not being nosy, and I'm not. I'm from Charlotte," Maggie said, smiling. "We moved to Kansas City a few years ago. We came down to visit my sister Angie and her husband this weekend, and we're staying at the Lodge."

"How nice!" Heidi said. "Would you like to join us for lunch?"

"Thanks, but I can't," Maggie said. "I'm on the way out to meet her in town right now. She must not know you, Dolly. I'm sure she would have told me if she did!"

They chatted for a few moments more and then said goodbye.

The next day, she was dead.

———◆———

The Sunday paper reported that Maggie Burns had been murdered. As Tim studied her photo on the front page, his muscles tensed and his throat tightened. She looked a whole lot like Dolly.

He wondered how his wife would react when she saw this. He had just brought the newspaper in, and she would be downstairs soon. He sat down at the table and read the article.

According to the reporter, Maggie and her husband had checked into the Lodge at Ardennes on Friday. The next evening, they had dinner there with her sister and brother-in-law. Afterward, Maggie went up to her hotel room and turned in early, and her husband went to his in-laws' house to play poker and ended up spending the night with them. When he got back to the hotel the next morning, he discovered his wife's naked body tied to the bed. Her arms and legs were bound with twine, and her mouth was sealed with duct tape. She had been strangled to death.

As Tim read on, his pulse quickened. Nobody staying at the Lodge said they heard any noises coming from the room. There were no security cameras anywhere and no security guard on the property. And as usual, nobody was at the front desk after eleven o'clock. All the entrances to the Lodge were locked at that hour and could be opened only with a key card. The police said there was no forced entry to the room, so the victim either knew the person who knocked on the door or thought she did.

There was no photo of a Barbie doll at the scene, but the murder fit the serial killer's MO.

Dolly walked into the kitchen just as Tim finished reading. None of the kids were up yet. "Babe," he said, "come over here and sit down with me, okay?"

She poured herself a cup of coffee and looked at him quizzically. "What is it?"

Dolly wasn't a morning person, and Tim knew this wasn't going to be good.

"Just come over here, okay?"

She sank into a chair, and her eyes fell on the headline. She stiffened. Her eyes widened, and her face went white. "I met that woman yesterday at the club, Tim! Heidi said she mistook her for me for a second and called her my doppelgänger. We talked to her before we had lunch."

He slid his arm around her shoulders as she finished reading. Then she turned and faced him. She was trembling. "People who know me are seeing this, and I'm sure they're thinking the same thing I am. If the murderer *was* the Barbie Killer, what if he's coming after me next?"

———◉———

They didn't have to wait very long to find out who the murderer was. Two days later, *The Huntington Post* published a handwritten note on the front page.

Stop all the whispers about me. I didn't have a chance to get a doll this time, but I killed Maggie. I had to because the demons won't rest. How many more must I kill before I get in the national news?

- The Barbie Killer

Chapter 19

Dolly changed her routine. She didn't go straight to the Athletic Club after dropping off the kids at school anymore. She did her errands at different times. She checked the phone for a dial tone when she walked in the door each time she got home. And she armed the security system not only when she left the house but when she was home alone.

The words *How many more must I kill* kept ringing in her ears. Her anxiety level skyrocketed, and she started getting headaches. She couldn't sleep at night, and constant fatigue was making her jumpy and cross. She was falling apart.

She didn't want to see a doctor and ask for a prescription for sleeping pills. She'd never taken them, and she was worried that they might cause her to walk in her sleep. She'd never seen a therapist about her sleepwalking or her phobias—in addition to bugs and superglue, she was afraid of attics and wouldn't go up in one. But she had to do something. She pulled out the phone book and found a therapist who could see her the next day. Her name was Clarice Prejean.

<hr>

Dolly's stomach was churning when she arrived at Clarice's office. She knocked on the door, and Clarice greeted her and ushered her in. Clarice wore her auburn hair in a messy bun, in sharp contrast to her tailored navy suit and mid-heel pumps. Dolly guessed that she was about ten years older than Dolly herself was, and something in her dark, hooded eyes suggested that she had seen more than her fair share of trauma.

Introductions and small talk over, Clarice asked Dolly to sit in a blue club chair. She sat in an identical one across from her.

"Now, what can I help you with, Dolly?"

Dolly wasn't sure where to begin, and despite her intention not to, she started rambling. Within a few minutes, she told Clarice she wasn't sleeping or eating, was anxious, and was getting occasional headaches.

"Have you seen your primary care doctor?"

"No. I don't want a prescription. I've been taking ibuprofen for my headaches."

"Not overdoing it, though, I hope."

"No."

"Okay. Have you lost any weight?"

"A little. It's just—I don't think the cause is physical. I've always been a little anxious."

Clarice wrinkled her brow. "But your anxiety level has been rising?"

"It has lately, yes."

"Why do you think that is?"

Dolly bit her lip and hesitated a few seconds before responding. "Honestly, I think it's because I look so much like the Barbie Killer's latest victim."

"The Barbie Killer?"

Dolly nodded. "The serial killer of Huntington. Didn't you see his note, published in the newspaper?"

"I don't get the paper, but I did hear about that. I haven't seen any pictures of the victim, so I didn't realize that she resembles you."

"She could almost have been my twin," said Dolly.

"My goodness. Go on, please."

Over the next few minutes, Dolly told her everything she'd learned, adding that before they arrived in Huntington, she and Tim didn't know that the Barbie Killer existed. She said she was afraid he would target her next.

"I think I understand now," Clarice said softly.

"So can you help me?"

"I'll certainly try. But first, let me get to know you a little. You mentioned earlier that you moved here to Huntington last summer?"

"In June. My husband was transferred here."

"Do you work?"

"I did, but I've been a stay-at-home mom for about ten years. We have three kids, and the youngest is in first grade this year."

"Well, I'm sure you stay very busy with three school-age children. Do you think you'll go back to work when they're older?"

"Maybe. Honestly, I'm enjoying the little time I have for myself at the moment. I don't know how I could fit a full-time or even a part-time job in and keep up with everything at home right now."

"Have you made some new friends here?"

"I have, yeah. I'm friends with a woman who moved here from Houston a few years ago. The rest are more like acquaintances than friends. Neighbors, other Hark wives, or both."

"What do you mean by 'Hark wives'?"

"Wives of Hark Industries executives. Like my husband, Tim."

"Tell me more about them."

Dolly shrugged. "I don't know them very well. I only met them because of Tim's job. They seem nice, though."

"You seem a little hesitant," Clarice said, tilting her head.

Dolly waited a few seconds before replying. "It's just—well, I'm annoyed and upset that none of them told me about the Barbie Killer. And that no one else did either."

"You think they should have?"

She nodded. "People who are from here, or who've been living here for a while, knew about him, and yes, I think they should have mentioned it."

"Do you feel a little betrayed?"

"I suppose so. I don't like to be kept in the dark, and I don't understand the silence."

"It *is* odd, I grant you. I think you'll find that people around here are like that, though. They mostly keep to themselves."

"So I've noticed."

Clarice cleared her throat. "Let's talk about your feelings of anxiety. Your fear that you may be targeted by the killer is quite logical. What concerns me is that it's adversely affecting you. It's preventing you from living a healthy life."

She wasn't telling Dolly anything she didn't know. "So tell me how I can keep it from doing that. What can I do to feel better and be healthy?"

"First, let's talk about the things that you can't change," she said. "It's a fact that the killer's last victim strongly resembled you. And you and your husband can't move away, right?"

"No. His job is here, and we don't have any other options right now."

"I see. So let's discuss what you *can* change—your own behavior and your attitude."

"Okay," Dolly said evenly, feeling a little miffed but curious.

"First, your behavior. Your actions and decisions."

"Okay. Go on."

Clarice lowered her chin and looked Dolly directly in the eye. "Even though you can't choose how others behave, you can choose your own behavior. You can decide not to live in fear, not to let the things you can't control have any power over you."

"It's that easy? I decide to do that, and it all goes away?"

"I'm not saying it's easy. It doesn't go away so much as you survive it. None of us can predict the future, influence fate, or alter anything that is out of our control."

"So what should I do? In practical terms?"

"Focus on your own personal safety. Do whatever you can to stay safe—but continue living your life, Dolly."

Dolly sat there in silence, slightly teary-eyed. Did Clarice realize just how difficult living her life was right now and that she was already doing the best she could to stay safe? Had she listened and understood when Dolly said that she feared the killer would come after her next?

"I'm saying you let the police find the serial killer," Clarice added, her tone firm yet more comforting than before. "All of us have to do that, and sooner or later, they will. For now, let's talk about some specific things that you can do to help you feel in control, okay?"

Clarice proposed a few practical ideas, and when the session was over, Dolly felt a bit better and was glad she came. On the way to the elevator, she noticed a petite dark-haired woman sitting in the waiting area. She had occasionally seen the woman in her step class. She was Barbara Isom's friend Shelly. Their eyes met, and Dolly gave her a slight nod. Perhaps Dolly wasn't the only woman in this town who was anxious and afraid.

She walked out of the building and climbed into the minivan. When she was two miles from home, the van suddenly started to shake. Hugging the steering wheel, she pulled over to the side of the road. Then she hopped out and was dismayed to see that she had a flat tire.

She didn't know how to change a tire, and she didn't want to try to learn. She and Tim didn't have AAA, but they had roadside assistance with their insurance company. The problem was that she would have to call them, and of course, there was no phone booth nearby. Even if she could get in touch with them, it would be a while before someone arrived to help her, and it was very cold. She knew she shouldn't drive on the flat the rest of the way home because it would do serious damage to the wheel. As she stepped back to her car door, a driver in a gray car pulled over behind her, got out of his car, and walked toward her.

But rather than feeling relieved that he was probably coming to her rescue, she felt a sudden pang of fear. He was a white middle-aged man and one of countless others who fit the general description of the Barbie Killer. If he was the killer, he would see her resemblance to his latest victim in a few seconds. What if he already knew, had been following her, and was looking for an opportunity like this to attack her? If she got out of the car, she would be alone with him and vulnerable, and he could overpower her and throw her into the trunk of his car.

That wasn't the Barbie Killer's MO, though. He broke into women's homes—or hotel rooms—and killed them there, in private. He didn't seize them off the street in broad daylight.

That didn't mean he wouldn't make an exception. She locked the doors. He stepped up to her window and knocked.

He's either a Good Samaritan or a criminal. But it was more likely that he was the former—and she had trusted two other strangers to come to her aid like this in the past—so she started the ignition so she could crack her window. If he threatened her or even spooked her in the least, she would drive away as fast as she could and not worry about the wheel.

"If you've got a jack and a spare, I can change it for you," he said, blowing on his hands clasped in front of his face. He was wearing sunglasses and a dark beanie.

"I do," she said cautiously. "Just a sec." They were stored under the floorboard in the back of the van. She unlocked the doors and popped the hatch open.

"You can stay there," he said. "I'll let you know when I'm done."

She rolled up the window, turned off the ignition, and watched him in the rear-view mirror. Exposed now, she felt even more defenseless. He hadn't displayed a moment of *déjà vu*, though, as if he recognized her face.

He got the jack and spare out immediately, shut the hatch, and got to work changing the tire. If anything went wrong, she could jump out of the car and run—or wave to any car passing by. Nothing did go wrong, though, and ten minutes later, he finished up and motioned to her. Holding her keys, she went over to take a look.

"Jack's back where it goes, and I laid your old tire in the back," he said with a smile. "Do you have very far to drive?"

Dolly shook her head. "Thank you so much."

"No problem. Good luck."

He walked over to his car, and she got into hers and locked the doors. She turned on the ignition but stayed where she was, watching him pull onto Web Road and turn right at the first light onto Anderson Road. The entrance to her neighborhood was past that light on the left. She pulled onto the road and glanced to the right as she passed under the light, and she didn't see him or any other cars in either direction.

Chapter 20

"There's a self-defense class for women at the YMCA," Dolly told Tim that evening. "I'd like to sign up for it, but I'll have to pay the non-member rate."

"Great idea," he said. "I wish I'd thought of that. Do it."

The Y had an evening self-defense class and an afternoon one. Dolly chose the afternoon one and was surprised to learn that she had filled the last open slot. The evening class was full and had a waiting list.

The Y was located in the East Side, a couple miles south of their neck of the woods. Cole played youth basketball there. When Dolly walked in a few minutes before one o'clock, her nose crinkled at the strong odor of sweat and grime. The industrial grade walls were a sickly shade of pale green, and large windows offered a view of the parking lot. The girl at the information counter had Dolly sign in and pointed toward the studio where the class would take place.

She supposed most women in this class of about twenty were members of the YMCA, but she spotted a few that she'd seen at the Athletic Club. Betsy and Susie from book club were there along with a woman named Lynn Grady, another mom from Audrey's dance class. The instructor, a trim, petite woman named Dana Marshall, started off by talking about prevention and awareness.

"The most important thing we can do to defend ourselves is to prevent the need to do so," she said. "To do that, we need to develop situational awareness. That means being aware of our surroundings, paying attention to warning signs, and noticing indicators of a possible attack."

She paused for a second and looked around the room. "For example," she continued, "when we're walking to and from our vehicles in a parking lot. When we're putting groceries in the car. When we're walking or running alone in a park. Basic, ordinary, everyday activities. The key is that, while we're busy doing them, we need to be aware of who is around us."

Dolly and several other women in the class nodded.

Dana smiled. "Sounds like common sense, right? Many of you are probably already doing this. If you're not, you should. However, it doesn't mean being paranoid or fearful. All it means is being alert and conscious of anyone who could pose a threat to your safety."

For the next several minutes, she led a discussion about how to do so and how to do it automatically. "When you're constantly aware of your surroundings, you'll feel safer and more empowered to protect yourself from any danger. So awareness is the first of three A's in self-defense, and it's key to avoiding violence.

"The second A is assessment, which means assessing and evaluating your environment, deciding if you feel at risk, and being ready to extricate yourself if you think you are. And the final A is action—actual self-defense moves. I'm going to teach you several, beginning with the basics. So I need a volunteer."

She looked around at those who had raised their hands and chose Lynn.

"Okay. You'll be the attacker, and I'll be the defender," Dana said. "Don't worry. I'll show you what to do, and I won't hurt you." Everyone laughed.

Lynn followed her example, and Dana demonstrated a simple move and then patiently explained how she did it. It was called a heel palm strike, where you used the heel of your dominant hand to jab up at the attacker's chin or nose. Then you recoiled your arm quickly, which would hopefully make the attacker stagger backward so you could escape.

Dana had everyone partner up to practice it, and Betsy was Dolly's partner. Dolly felt a little clumsy and hesitant at first, but as they kept trying, she felt more comfortable doing the move. Over the next twenty minutes, Dana made her way around the room to watch and to give tips and feedback. Then she taught the group a couple of other simple moves.

"You've all done well for your first time," Dana said at the end of class. "You have to practice, though. As they say in dance—and self-defense *is* kind of a dance—practice is the key to knowledge. So over the coming weeks, you should practice at home. We'll be learning more moves here and getting more comfortable with them over time too."

She raised her hand. "Now, one last thing before we go—and this is important and something you need to wrap your heads around. We all have a natural tendency not to want to hurt another person. It's just who we are as humans, right? And as women. But if someone attacks us, we have to behave the *opposite* way. We have to *want* to hurt our attacker so we can stop him. Sometimes—and I don't want to scare you—that may mean that *we* get hurt in the process. For instance, we could hurt our hand when we hit back. We could injure an arm or elbow, maybe badly. But remember this. Getting injured is much better than dying." She paused and looked around the room. "Next time, we'll talk about gut instincts, intuition, and how to adopt defense moves into what's called our muscle memory."

⸻ ● ⸻

The next afternoon, when Dolly walked to her car with a shopping cart full of groceries, she found a folded piece of yellow paper stuck under her windshield wiper. She pulled it off, thinking it was a flyer asking for a donation or an advertisement, and tossed it in the car. After unloading her groceries and putting the cart away, she got in the car, put her purse down, picked up the flyer and opened it. It was a type-written note.

I've been dreaming of you and watching you. Soon, I'll be waiting for you.

"What the hell?" she muttered.

Beads of sweat popped on the back of her neck, and her body stiffened. *Situational awareness.* She jerked her head around, scanning the parking lot. No one was looking at her. Was someone crouched right behind her seat in the car? She whirled around and looked. No one was there.

Was the note only a prank? Or did the killer write it and leave it there for her?

She tried to calm down but kept checking her mirrors and looking at other drivers on the way home. After checking the phone for a dial tone, she called Tim at work.

"I'll be right there," he said.

As far as Dolly knew, the Barbie Killer had never written creepy notes to his victims before he attacked them. But that didn't mean he didn't write this one. Since it wasn't an actual threat, telling the police about it would probably be futile, though.

Minutes later, Tim walked in the door. "Are you all right?" he asked as he wrapped his arms around her.

"I'm okay." She buried her forehead in his shoulder. "What if the killer is stalking me and he left me that note?"

Tim pulled her closer then shifted his hands to her shoulders and looked her in the eye. "Then changing your routine and being more careful when you go out isn't going to matter," he said. "Knowing self-defense is great, but that may not be enough. It's time we bought a gun."

She shut her eyes for a second. *He's right.*

Tim continued, "We'll find a secure place to keep it and where the kids won't be able to find it. I'll figure out what kind to get and where, and then we need to learn how to use it."

"Okay," she said. "I agree, and I don't think we have a choice."

The next day after lunch, he drove to a gun store and picked out a handgun. The dealer ran a quick background check on him, and there was no waiting period.

Chapter 21

He drove to the Toys R Us store and made his way over to the pink aisles. If anyone asked, he was buying a Barbie doll for his niece for her birthday. No one would ask, though. Barbies flew off the shelves here. The only toys that were more popular were the Beanie Babies that McDonald's handed out free with every Happy Meal.

But Barbie dolls were expensive and had gotten more expensive over time. Used to be, he could pick one up for a couple of bucks and there were only a few different models. Back when he'd started, you could get a blond or a brunette Barbie. She had a little sister named Skipper and a best friend, Midge. They didn't come with anything except a simple dress. Now, they came in big boxes dressed in fancy outfits. There was Workout Barbie, Olympic Skater Barbie, Holiday Barbie, and even Dentist Barbie, to name only a few. He looked for the least fussy one and would choose her for her hair color. Today, he needed a brunette. He hadn't had time to get one earlier, but better late than never. He picked up an Arctic Barbie, but she was a little pricey, so he kept looking.

These Barbie dolls with their plastic smiles and unrealistic figures were good symbols of his missions. The more recent ones were newcomers to town, prancing around with their made-up faces masking criticism of and annoyance with Midwesterners. They brought their big-city, haughty attitudes with them and thought they were better than other people.

He finally found the least expensive model, a basic brunette Barbie doll, and ambled to the checkout counter. The clerk mumbled a greeting and barely noticed him. He paid with cash.

"Have a nice day," the girl with the dark-red hair mumbled.

"Same to you," he said as he turned to the exit.

In the parking lot, he took the doll out of her box and threw the box into a trash can.

<hr>

There was a reason why Maggie and Dolly looked so much alike, and he wanted to know what it was. There had to be a connection, and for the life of him, he was dying to discover it.

He had to get inside the Garner house.

The following week, he found his opportunity. Dolly went on a field trip with one of her kids' classes and was going to be out all day. It was easy to break into the house. He got in through the sliding door in the kitchen that opened onto the back patio. Those had always been easy to jimmy because they were secured with cheap latches, not real locks. And most people, including the Garners, didn't barricade their sliding doors by placing a metal rod at the bottom like they should.

All he needed was a short crowbar, and he was in.

He slid the door shut, disarmed the security system, and got to work. The first thing he did was start looking for a fireproof safe. Almost everyone in their socio-economic class had one. He had one. What he was looking for was Dolly's passport. That would show her date of birth and her maiden name. He knew Maggie's maiden name was Cunningham because although it wasn't on her driver's license, it had been in her obituary.

What's the probability that Dolly's maiden name is Cunningham? It seemed rather slim. Then again, the idea that the two women weren't blood related seemed unlikely. It might be impossible to find out, however. If they were related, though, Dolly would have gone to the funeral in Kansas City.

He headed to the basement and went into the unfinished storage room, where he found several boxes and plastic containers but no safe. That made sense since the Garners weren't from around here. Huntington residents knew to store their valuables in the basement in case a tornado hit their house. Newcomers often stored them in the master bedroom or a closet. He climbed the two flights of stairs up to the master and looked around.

Voilà. A gray safe, a strongbox, sat on a shelf in her large walk-in closet. Her husband had an identical closet. The key was in the lock. Typical, he thought. He flipped it open and rifled through the contents, looking for anything listing her maiden name.

He didn't see her passport, but he found something else just as good—their marriage license. Her maiden name wasn't Cunningham. It was Wilson. That didn't prove anything. Maybe one or both of the women had been adopted by a stepfather and had taken his name. It was far-fetched but possible.

He put the marriage license back in the safe and closed it. There was no need to wipe it for prints, but he did it anyway, out of habit. Then he walked into the huge master bathroom and over to the bathtub, under a picture window overlooking the front yard. He took a risk and peeked through the wood blinds.

No one was out there, so he let his gaze linger for a moment. The view almost mesmerized him. He hadn't been this close to where that murder had happened in decades. But here he was now, in the house built on the piece of land where it had. He hadn't planned to be here that night, and he had often wondered about the impact it had on his life.

Because he was sure that it had altered him, and he believed in the butterfly effect. The future was shaped by all the things that happened daily—not just the big ones but the little ones, even the miniscule and seemingly unimportant ones. It was shaped not just by actions but by words. Words people said and those that they left unsaid.

Soon after that awful night, the demons got ahold of him. They got into his brain and wouldn't leave. He tried to control them, and at times, he succeeded. But the monsters in his head always won in the end. He had to do their bidding. He didn't think of himself as evil, though. He was at the mercy of something outside of himself, something that he couldn't conquer alone. Maybe he should have asked somebody for help a long time ago. But he had been afraid they would laugh at him, or worse, that they would have him sent to an insane asylum.

He shuddered and backed away from the window. He simply couldn't let his mind go there. If he did, he would slip into the past and he might not be able to get out. And the past was too dangerous.

He needed to refocus on the task at hand. He glanced around. *What else can I look for that will shed light on why Dorothy Wilson Garner so closely resembles Margaret Cunningham Burns? Are the two women not related by blood at all, and this is only a coincidence, an oddity for which there is no explanation?*

It was maddening.

He didn't believe in coincidences, though. He believed in logic and in things that made sense. He believed in explanations and in reason. There was a reason for everything, and if you looked hard enough, you could generally find it. But whatever it was, he might not succeed at finding it today.

He searched the rest of the closet, the bathroom, and the master bedroom. He opened every drawer and was careful not to disturb anything. He didn't want to spook Dolly or her husband, not today anyway. Finding nothing, he descended to the main level and began looking around in the kitchen. He searched the cabinets and every drawer, nook, and cranny but found nothing. The built-in desk in the kitchen didn't yield anything either. Then he went into the den. There were built-in cabinets and shelves on either side of a brick fireplace. He opened a cabinet door and discovered three large boxes full of photographs.

He opened each one and thumbed through the pictures, which weren't organized or in any particular order. This time, he wasn't so careful about what he touched. It wasn't necessary, nor was wiping his fingerprints. After ten minutes of searching, he found some old photos of a teenage or young adult Dolly. In some, she was with another girl, maybe a friend or a family member. He didn't find any of her with another girl who looked like her.

The mystery would have to go unsolved, at least for now. Maybe it was just a fluke that the two women looked alike. Nature had its own rules. Maybe there was a man out there who looked very much like him too. He turned and left the house the same way he had gotten in. When Dolly came home later today, she wouldn't notice anything amiss since nothing was.

Chapter 22

The storm hit after dinner, and the city issued a tornado warning. Dolly and Tim and the kids scrambled down to the basement, piled onto the sofa, and turned on the Weather Channel. The children were unconcerned and quickly got bored, but their parents watched intently and breathed a sigh of relief when the storm passed without incident.

Tim and Dolly made love that night, and afterward, she found it hard to drift off, which was unusual because sex usually had a relaxing effect on her. Thoughts and worries about the Barbie Killer swirled in her head, and she tossed and turned as Tim slept beside her.

The next thing she knew, she woke up in his walk-in closet. She looked around and realized she was standing directly under the trapdoor to the attic. Had she been about to pull it down and climb up there? The memory of hiding in the attic during a game of hide-and-seek as a child—and not being able to get out—made her shudder.

"Dolly, it's me. Let's get back in bed," Tim said softly in her ear.

He was right beside her, his arms at his sides. Hers were crossed in front of her chest. The closet door was partially lit by a lamp in the bedroom, and the overhead light was off. She looked up at the trapdoor and trembled.

"What happened?" she asked.

"I heard a noise and went to look for you." He started guiding her slowly toward the bed.

"What noise?"

"It was a thud. Maybe you dropped that." He pointed to a large photo album on the floor. She kept her albums on a shelf in her closet. She must have picked up this one and ended up in here for some reason.

"You must have been sleepwalking," he said, easing her into bed.

She lay down, and he slid in beside her. She let out a deep breath and closed her eyes. She hated the out-of-control feeling she had after walking in her sleep. Why had she grabbed the photo album?

Maybe she'd been looking for a baby photo of Hugh because his homeroom was having a baby picture contest. It was one of many spring activities celebrating the seventh graders as they prepared to move up to their final year at the school next fall. But his baby pictures wouldn't be in that album. They would be in a box she kept in a cabinet in the den, along with photos of her and Tim when they were young and first married.

The next day, she pulled out the box and chose a good picture of Hugh. She'd ask if he approved, of course. She didn't want to embarrass him, which, at his age, was fairly easy to do. Then she noticed a few photos of herself as a teenager mixed in with the ones of Hugh. *Did he rifle through them and mix these with the ones of him?* If he had beaten her to it and had already picked out another photo, that was fine. She just had to make sure he brought one in.

That evening after school, she asked him about it.

"No, I don't know where to look for one," he said. "I need it by Monday, though."

⸺⬤⸺

The next day at self-defense class, Dolly's partner was her friend Lynn. They often saw each other dropping off and picking up the girls at the dance studio and usually stopped to chat.

Lynn lived in a nearby neighborhood, but she and her husband, Warren, didn't fit into the mold of typical East Siders. Warren didn't work at Hark, Lynn had a part-time job at their church, and their two children went to public school.

Dana came over to watch the two of them practice a maneuver they had just learned to use if an attacker grabbed them by the wrist. The move was to use your free hand to twist his other hand down very hard to try to break his grip and push him away.

"Okay, Lynn, you be the attacker first. Then switch roles," Dana said and stood back to watch. "That's right. Be firm and fast. Don't hesitate. Speed is your friend. It may feel awkward or uncomfortable at first, but at a certain point, once you've done it enough, muscle memory will take over."

They did it again. "Much better," she said and then went on to watch the next couple.

When the forty-five-minute class ended, Dana congratulated everyone on their progress.

"Don't forget to practice your moves at home," she called as they began to file out.

"Thanks, Dana," Dolly said as Dana smiled and waved goodbye.

She and Lynn walked to the parking lot with Betsy and Susie. Dolly introduced them to Lynn.

"I sure hope all of this is sinking in," Betsy said. "I always feel pretty good when I leave here, but then I worry that I'd panic and forget it all if something happened."

"I'm afraid of that too," Dolly said.

"Same here," Lynn said. "Honestly, though, I don't want to find out."

"It doesn't come naturally to me," Susie said. "I go over everything at home and practice."

"Well, see you next week," said Betsy. They left, and Lynn and Dolly lingered to talk a bit more.

"I hope we learn what to do if we're attacked from behind," Dolly said.

Lynn gave her a look, her eyes wide. "I hope so too. I'm terrified of the Barbie Killer. I don't go out at night anymore. I quit my bunco group, and I make Warren look around outside and double-check the locks every night."

"Why is everyone so afraid to talk about him? We've lived here almost a year, and no one ever mentioned him to us."

Lynn glanced to her left and right. They were standing in between their cars, and no one else was around. "I've lived here all my life, and I think it's because people are superstitious. People may whisper about him, but most don't like to talk about him because they think they'll jinx themselves if they do—and that if he hears people talking about him, it could inspire him to strike again. One time, about eight years ago, the paper ran a story about him on the sixth anniversary of his last murder. Two days later, he killed someone else."

"The woman whose boyfriend he stabbed but who survived?"

"Right," said Lynn, her eyes wide again. "How did you know that?"

"I went through old newspapers in the archives at the library. The article said he couldn't identify the killer. Even though it's been so long, I'd like to meet him and ask him what he remembers."

Lynn shook her head. "He died of cancer a few years ago."

"Oh, that's sad," Dolly said and then sighed.

"Well, but it sounds like you did your homework," Lynn said. "After the paper published that note from the killer a few months ago, I think a lot of people have been afraid that it would spur him on to kill again. I know I've been. Fear is what is making people keep quiet about him, Dolly. Once the police find him, they'll start talking, I bet."

"*If* the police find him," she said.

Dolly hadn't told Lynn or anyone else except Tim and Clarice about the note on her windshield. She had thought about going to the police but decided they wouldn't do anything about it, and really, what could they do? But if it was written by the killer—if he was *watching* her—then Dolly was doing what other Huntington residents had done for years when it came to the killer and his victims. She was keeping quiet. For now.

"So, are your boys going to Scout camp in June?" Lynn asked.

"I'm not sure. We haven't signed them up for it yet."

"Well, you better do it soon if they want to go. It fills up fast," Lynn said.

"Really? This early?"

Lynn nodded. "Paul loves it. Warren usually volunteers at it, but he's been too busy at work lately, so he had to pass this year. I'm pretty sure he's got all of Paul's old pinewood derby cars out in his shed, along with his tools and yard stuff."

"So many people have sheds here," Dolly remarked. "We don't, and no one I knew in Georgia did either."

She had noticed that Tim's boss and some of his colleagues had backyard sheds. So did many other East Siders—and West Siders, too, for that matter. Tim kept his lawn equipment in the garage, and they had an unfinished storage room in the basement where they stored Christmas decorations and other miscellaneous items.

Lynn smiled. "I guess it's a Midwestern thing. Lots of people here have them, even rich folks, and you wouldn't believe all the stuff they keep in them. Warren likes to tinker in ours when he's puttering around."

Chapter 23

The next morning, Max walked into Tim's office and quietly shut the door.

"A buddy of mine at the police department just told me that Roger's been identified as a person of interest in the murder of Maggie Burns," he said.

Tim lifted his eyebrows. "Whoa. What does that mean?"

Max grimaced. "Basically, that he's a suspect—unofficially—but that they don't have enough to charge him with a crime. But my buddy said the police have reason to believe that he knew her."

Tim blew out a breath. "Did he say why?"

Max nodded. "Off the record, they found an item at the scene with Roger's initials on it."

"What, a handkerchief or something?"

"I don't know. He wouldn't tell me. But I wonder if they have something else on him. The police can't bring him in for questioning, but they can ask him lots of questions and hope that he answers and cooperates with them," Max said. "He doesn't have to, though, but I'm sure he will. That is, unless he has something to hide."

"You don't think..."

Max shrugged. "I don't know. Anyway, just wanted you to know."

As Max headed back toward his office, Tim lingered at the door to his. Tamara Weeks, one of the department secretaries, walked at a brisk pace down the corridor in the other direction, wearing her typical stern expression. She glanced at Tim, and he gave her a slight nod, shut his door, and sat down at his desk to digest the news.

If Roger knew the victim, how did they meet and what was their relationship?

That weekend, it was Tim and Dolly's turn to host a Hark game night. Roger and Mary Ellen couldn't make it, but Max and Glenda and Joe and his wife, Diane, were coming. As a group of six, the plan was to play bunco, a dice game. Four people would play as two teams at a head table. The other two people were going to play against each other and rotate with the losing team at the head table. It was a simple, fun-but-mindless game and perfect for drinking and socializing. The two couples arrived at the same time, and Joe knocked on the door.

"Welcome to our home," Tim said and ushered them inside.

After cocktails were served, they all sat down in the living room to chat before getting started. As often happened, the men settled into their own conversation, and the women talked to each other. They were all aware of Roger's situation, but nobody mentioned it or speculated about him. Just as Tim was finishing his drink, the wives brought up an upcoming event to be held in May called the Riverfest.

"Some of my book club friends mentioned it recently," Dolly said to the ladies. "What is the Riverfest, and when is it?"

The men stopped talking and began watching and listening to their wives.

"It's sort of like a state fair," Glenda said. "It's held every year in early May."

"It's very Midwestern, Dolly," Diane added. Several years younger than Joe, she was a tall blonde with close-set eyes and a narrow face. "It's actually smaller than a state fair, but it's well attended. They block off an area downtown west of the river and have amusement park rides, an arcade, face painting—that kind of thing."

"Yes," Glenda said. "Some people bring coolers and blankets and sit on the riverbank to watch the fireworks on Saturday night."

"Fireworks?" Dolly said. "So it's a celebration of some kind?"

"Not really," said Diane. "But it's a Huntington tradition."

"And a rare chance for West Siders to mix with East Siders," Joe put in. "The *hoi polloi* rub elbows—literally—with the *muckety-mucks*." He chuckled.

"The riffraff mingle with the elite," Max translated for Dolly and made a face. Glenda gave him a side-eye look.

"I wouldn't really call it mingling," Joe corrected him. "In fact, Hark people rarely go to it." He shot a glance at Tim and then looked at Dolly.

"We went last year," Glenda admitted. "I'm not sure if we will this time."

"Most East Siders don't," Joe continued. "It's kind of a gathering of the great unwashed, for lack of a better term. Just not our kind of thing."

"You're such a snob, Joe," Diane said teasingly. "It can be fun for the kids," she said to Dolly. "If yours like amusement parks, they'd probably enjoy it."

"Another round?" Tim asked. Everyone nodded, and Dolly joined him in the kitchen.

When they returned a few minutes later with a tray of drinks, Joe and Max were talking about their plans to play golf the following weekend.

For a few seconds, Tim wondered why they hadn't asked him to join them. They seemed to like and enjoy his company, at work and otherwise. But even though he often played with Max or Roger at Ardennes, neither they nor Joe had invited him to any major golf outings or to play in tournaments at other clubs. At times, it felt like they were holding him at arm's length, outside of a professional inner circle to which he wasn't welcome. He was well regarded at work and very good at his job, but although Joe had assured him that he would be, he'd never been introduced to Peter Hark or to any other top executives. Tim wasn't sure if Max had been, but it was common knowledge that Roger often met with the CEO and socialized with him and his team.

After their guests left that night, Tim asked Dolly if she wanted to take the kids to the Riverfest.

"Let's ask them if they want to go," she said. "I think they might like it. Celeste told me she and Bob were going with their two kids. Heidi said they're going too."

"Well, that's two East Siders," Tim said. "And one of them is a Hark family." He winked at her. "We'll make two."

Dolly shook her head. "That sounds so strange. A 'Hark family.' As if it's a club or something." *No, not "as if"—it* is *a club, and a bizarre one at that, and we aren't members.* "But yeah, Celeste's husband works for some other company."

"If the kids want to go, I don't see the harm," Tim said. He and Dolly were always on the lookout for kid-friendly, inexpensive activities anyway.

"I agree. It might be fun, and I could use some wholesome fun family time."

Chapter 24

Dolly arrived ten minutes early for her next self-defense class and saw Dana standing in the front of the studio, talking to a fellow student whose name Dolly didn't know.

"I'm paralyzed with fear about him," the woman said to Dana, "and if he attacks me, I'm worried that I won't remember anything from class and won't be able to protect myself."

Dolly lingered in the back of the room, unsure whether to leave the room or not.

"I totally understand, and I'm sure a lot of other women in this town feel the same way," Dana said softly. She looked over at Dolly and motioned for her to join them.

"I'd be lying if I said I wasn't afraid of him too," Dana said as Dolly approached. "But I know that learning self-defense helps us deal with our fear. We shouldn't underestimate ourselves either. Trust me—each new move you learn is seeping into your consciousness."

Dana laid a hand on the other woman's arm and looked back and forth at her and Dolly as she continued, "I grew up in an abusive home, with a violent stepfather who beat my mother and me. She didn't have the strength to leave him, so she tiptoed around him, and so did I. I was constantly frightened of him and angry at her, and I left home as soon as I could. Eventually, I learned self-defense, got a degree in psychology, and became a domestic violence and abuse counselor. When Mom finally left him, I realized that having courage doesn't mean that you don't have fear."

"Wow. Thank you so much for sharing your story," Dolly said.

Dana said, "I wanted you to know because I want both of you to believe in yourselves. A lot of people have survived domestic abuse, and it's not the same as coming face to face with a killer. But both take courage and the will to survive."

The door to the studio opened, and several other students entered the room and took their places. After greeting everyone, Dana announced that they would learn the maneuvers to use if an attacker took his victim by surprise and crept up on her from behind.

"Even though your muscle memory and your gut instinct will automatically kick in," she began, "we still have to know what to do to survive such an attack."

Dolly and Lynn exchanged glances, and everyone nodded.

"Okay. Let's say the attacker suddenly grabs me from behind. My instinct is to break his grip to get away from him, and I need to create distance so that I can escape. But if he has a strong hold on me, and if he tries to choke me, I only have a few seconds before I lose all my strength and pass out. Then it's over. But instead of letting that happen, here's what I can do."

She looked around the room and motioned to Betsy to come forward and join her. "You be the attacker," she said, and Betsy stood behind her and placed her hands gently around Dana's throat.

"I can kick him or stomp on his foot, like this." Dana demonstrated the move, raising her knee and sending her heel down and back toward Betsy's foot but missing it on purpose. "Or I can drop my center of gravity—I can squat—which will make it very hard for him to keep me in his grip. If I can't do that, I can use an elbow to try to hit him in the belly or to strike him in the face." Dana did the moves slowly, not touching Betsy but almost. "What I need to do then is quickly twist my torso around to face him to try to break his hold and get away. And if I can't do *that*, I can kick him in the groin or jab a finger into his eye."

She looked around the room and continued, "If he keeps coming at me—and he might—I'll use my hands to hit him hard, right in the face." She demonstrated by punching and slapping at an imaginary attacker. "I'm gonna keep ripping into his face nonstop, and then as soon as I can, I'm going to run away from him. Now, I know this is a lot to remember, but after you practice these moves over and over, they'll come to you."

They paired up to practice, and Dana went around the room to watch each couple, have them trade places, and offer tips and feedback.

Afterward, she said to the group, "You're doing great. Remember, when you hurt him, you may get hurt too. So don't forget what I said. Getting injured is much better than dying."

At the end of class, Dolly felt more confident but still had some nagging doubts. Learning how to defend herself was a good thing, but it forced her to envision the worst. If that moment came, would she freeze? Or would the will to survive save her?

Chapter 25

Saying that he was anxious to clear his name and assert his innocence, Roger cooperated with the police and answered their questions. Although he was a corporate attorney who dealt primarily with legal contracts, some of his associates were criminal defense lawyers and prosecuting attorneys, and he knew that police had every right to lie to people and often did. He also knew that the police didn't like it at all when people lied to them.

But he lied to them anyway and said he had been at home alone the night of the murder.

It wasn't a solid alibi because Mary Ellen and the kids had been away that weekend on a ski trip. But he didn't worry about that because no one could prove that he wasn't home or that he was at the Lodge. The police said they found a money clip with his initials on it in the hotel room, but that was circumstantial evidence. Lots of other people had Roger's initials, and there was no proof that the money clip belonged to him.

Then they told Roger that an employee at the Lodge had come forward saying that she had seen him enter the victim's room around ten o'clock that night.

So he told them the truth. He had been romantically involved with the woman, the money clip belonged to him, and he had said that he was home that night because he didn't want his wife to learn of his affair. However, he insisted that he left around eleven o'clock. No one saw him leave, though, which implied that he could have been at the crime scene at the time of the murder, so now he was more than just a person of interest. He was a suspect in a homicide case.

Everyone at the office was stunned by the news, and no one could believe that he was guilty. If Roger *had* killed her, then he was the Barbie Killer—unless the real killer was claiming credit for a murder he hadn't committed.

In Tim's mind, the idea that Roger was the town serial killer defied every single strand of logic. The Barbie Killer was depraved, vicious, and evil. Everything that Roger was not. He was well-liked and respected, and his competitive and assertive nature was tempered by a genuine affability. He was known as a man's man yet also that rare version of one who was terribly ambitious but still a gentleman.

But—what if he actually is *the Barbie Killer?*

It sounded far-fetched, yet it was possible. Roger was about the right age. He had grown up in Huntington, and he knew it like the back of his hand. He was an outdoorsman and liked working with his hands. He'd been in the service when he was young, and he knew how to handle a weapon.

Roger was an intelligent man. Although he was courteous to everyone, he was a typical Midwesterner—reserved, thoughtful, and a bit circumspect, almost as if he was hiding something. And he was known to be assertive, aggressive, and even sneaky at times. But wasn't that the definition of a good lawyer? Tim had seen the way that Roger behaved in enough corporate meetings not to underestimate his professional talents. He did his job, he worked long hours, and he got results. And results were what Hark was all about.

Long hours. Those two words now took on a whole new meaning. If Roger hadn't been in the office working nights and weekends as he claimed, then he'd had the time to plan and commit murders. Tim suddenly recalled something Roger said to him shortly after he started at the company.

"If you have to leave the office," he'd advised, *"lay your suit jacket over the back of your chair. That way, people will think you're still working and that you're just somewhere else in the building."*

Or maybe you were somewhere else in the town.

———⊙———

Dolly didn't want to believe that Roger was the killer, but if he was, then the nightmare would be over. He would be tried and go to jail for life. He might even get the death penalty.

"Mary Ellen must be devastated," Dolly said as she and Tim got ready for bed that night. "To find out your husband is cheating on you is bad enough, but a murderer?"

"I can't believe he's the Barbie Killer," Tim said, now in his T-shirt and shorts, "especially since she was his mistress. The killer could have gotten there minutes after he left that night. And what about that note in the paper? *The demons won't rest?* Roger's a smart guy. The guy who wrote that note isn't."

"He's smart enough not to get caught for decades."

"And lucky enough," Tim said.

Dolly wasn't sure that Roger hadn't written the note. Maybe he was the killer and he had worded it that way on purpose because he enjoyed messing around with the press and the police. Maybe Roger had left that note on her windshield and was planning to kill her next.

Roger could have been leading a double life for decades, disguising the person that he really was. And who knew what really went on inside of someone's head anyway?

And—don't we all act like someone other than our true self, every single day of our lives?

———⊙———

The rumor going around at the office was that Roger had been cheating on his wife for months. If that was true, it seemed even more puzzling to Tim than shocking.

How did he have the time? Roger was always at the office—or so people thought—when he wasn't with his family, and he worked long hours, even weekends, to support them. Had he spent his weekends with his girlfriend in Kansas City and told his wife that he was working?

The fact that Maggie looked so much like Dolly was rather creepy. Was that why Roger had done a double take when he met Dolly at the party last summer? Although Tim and Roger socialized with each other and worked together, Tim realized that he didn't really know the man. But he was still shocked by what he'd heard. He'd had the impression that Roger wasn't like other men that he had worked with—men who routinely hit on women when away on business, had casual sex, and didn't think anything of it. As far as Tim knew, Roger didn't go on business trips. He worked in Huntington, where everyone knew everyone, and everyone knew everything *about* everyone.

Or thought they did.

Tim loved his wife, had never considered being unfaithful to her, and didn't understand why some men like Roger chose to risk destroying their marriages and families by having an affair. Perhaps his marriage was quite different from Tim's. But weaving lies around a hidden relationship with a mistress just wasn't worth it and must be an awful way to live. But if the rumor was true, then Roger had done it.

But the idea that he had been seeing another woman for months, had murdered her, *and* had been stalking, attacking, and killing other women in this town for many years seemed preposterous.

Unless Roger was a monster.

Chapter 26

"Roger is no longer a suspect," Tim told Dolly when he got home one night that week.

The kids were playing in the backyard, and she had just started to make a salad for dinner. She wheeled around from the sink and met his eyes. Hers looked tired.

She hesitated for a second before replying. "That's great. Why?"

Tim set his briefcase down on the kitchen desk. "You didn't hear?"

She shook her head and leaned back against the counter, bracing herself but hoping for good news. Maybe they had finally found the real Barbie Killer and arrested him.

"A woman was found murdered in her home and had been killed while Roger was at the police station. A photo of a Barbie was next to her body."

Dolly's hand flew to her mouth. "Who was it? Where?"

"Dana Marshall, in Bonneville."

She gasped. "Oh my God. She was my self-defense instructor!" She started trembling.

He grabbed her shoulder, pulled her to him, and held her tightly. "Oh no, babe. I had no idea."

After a moment, she looked up at him. "Now, he's killed someone I *know*, Tim. Someone who knows—knew—how to defend herself."

"He must have surprised her—"

"Even so, she would have fought him off." Her eyes were brimming with tears. "She was petite, but she was strong. And she knew exactly what to do. I didn't know her that well, but I liked her, Tim. I felt more confident and safer after learning what she taught me."

The two of them had separated a little, facing each other, and his right arm was around her. He gently pushed a strand of her hair back from her face with his left hand.

She wiped away a tear. "And now—well, if he can kill a woman like Dana, I can't... I don't know."

"I don't know the details. I just heard this on the local radio station. Was she married?"

"I don't know. I don't think so," Dolly said. "I never saw her wear a wedding ring."

"Maybe she lived alone, and somehow he got in and quickly over-powered her."

"He must have done it really fast before she knew he was there. She was in great shape, and she was smart. I felt like she was an expert in self-defense."

"I'm sure she was. But he knows what he's doing, too, and on average, men are stronger than women—even strong women like her. The cops don't really know how old he is anyway. He could be in his mid-forties or even a little younger." He picked up his briefcase. "Babe, I'm going up to get changed. Then let's sit down and talk some more about it before dinner, okay?"

She nodded and turned to the counter to chop some tomatoes. She felt numb and suddenly very tired. How could the killer have crept up on a woman like Dana, who was so attuned to danger and was so skilled in self-defense? All of her experience and training hadn't saved her in the end. It just didn't make any sense. And it frightened Dolly.

She finished chopping and looked out the kitchen window. The boys were shooting hoops in their newly acquired basketball goal—she and Tim had bought it to encourage them to spend more time playing at home rather than at the park—and Audrey was blowing soap bubbles from a plastic container. They would hear about this murder too—at least Hugh would and probably Cole. They knew Dolly took a self-defense class but didn't know the name of her instructor. At the right time, she and Tim would sit down, tell them, and talk about it.

Even though the Barbie Killer was still out there, Dolly was relieved that Roger wasn't the killer and that he had been released. Now that his wife knew he had been unfaithful, their marriage was probably going to end, though. If their marriage turned out to be collateral damage in the quest to stop the Barbie Killer, that would really be a shame. Then again, some couples somehow survived infidelity. Perhaps it was more common than Dolly realized. No one knew what really went on in other people's marriages anyway.

Tim came downstairs a few minutes later and poured them both a glass of wine. They sat down in the den. "Maybe he killed Dana because she was teaching self-defense," he said. "Maybe he saw her as some kind of threat. But we can't paralyze ourselves by worrying about things we don't know and we can't control—"

Dolly bristled. "You know, the more I hear that said, the more I think it's bullshit. What are we *supposed* to worry about, then? Only what we *can* control?"

Tim started. "Babe. I-I only mean—"

"Look. If I can control something, I don't worry about it, Tim. I just control it. I take care of it. It's what I *can't* control or take care of that causes me to worry. That's the *definition* of worry for me—not being able to do anything about what frightens or upsets me."

Tim reached for her hand. "I love you, Dolly. I know that you worry. I just want you to feel protected. I don't want you to be anxious or afraid."

"How can I not be, when the victims' lives keep brushing closer and closer to my own?"

And if Dana couldn't escape the Barbie Killer, what chance do I have?

Chapter 27

He hadn't killed Maggie because she was Dolly's twin. He'd done it because she deserved it—and she was a dry run, a sort of dress rehearsal, for Dolly.

The mission in the hotel room had been different from the rest. It was the first one he had done in a public place or at least in a semi-public one. Hotel rooms were protected by privacy laws. Whatever you did inside them was your own business. And the reason for that mission was different from the others.

It had worked out okay, but he hadn't planned it very well. Instead of taking his time, he'd been rather hasty and had seized his opportunity. It was contrary to his usual way, so it bothered him a little and had put him on tilt. However, he'd been flexible yet deliberate, and he had done everything carefully and masterfully. He'd had to. And no matter what anybody might end up saying—if they ever found out—he hadn't chosen her at random. He'd seen her with her husband, and then he saw her lover enter and leave her hotel room late at night. He had picked her because she had committed adultery, which was a sin.

He had never been unfaithful to his wife. At least, not in the true meaning of the word. His missions didn't qualify as adultery because sex wasn't the point. Murder was. He and his wife were more like companions than lovers anyway, and they always had been. After the kids came along, they didn't have much sex, but he didn't mind. When he completed a mission, the sexual part provided a release, but it was only a by-product, like masturbating on his victims' clothing or while looking at porn. It was just something necessary and not sacred. As the politicians said, "It's only sex," and for him, it wasn't even that. It wasn't lovemaking. It was more like the opposite. The important things were the suffering and the death.

The adrenaline rush was his reward for obeying the demons. He wasn't addicted to that feeling, not like he had been when he was young. But it was refreshing to feel his pulse quicken, his heart pump faster, and his strength increase, even if just for a time. It excited him, and he wondered how he had managed to go so long without it.

Maggie's resemblance to Dolly was still an unsolved mystery. He could live with that. Some people looked very much alike, and these two women weren't identical. Nonetheless, because of their resemblance, the demons were pushing him more and more toward Dolly. She had been on his radar for a while anyway, and now, she was a walking reminder of Maggie's sin and had to be eliminated. Otherwise, the demons wouldn't let him rest.

He hadn't tried to frame Roger Stillwell for the murder, but he was pleased that Roger had been suspected. Even though the guy had been cleared, his wife would never trust him again and would probably divorce him. His life would fall apart, and he might even lose his job. But she would be better off without him. She would get a lot of his money, and he would land on his feet. Guys like him always did. And if that meant that he had to move away from Huntington, so be it.

Good riddance.

After the murder of Dana Marshall, his wife had taken the kids with her to Prairie City to stay with her mom for the weekend. She said she was terrified of the killer and needed to get away for a day or two. He knew she was perfectly safe, although he couldn't exactly convince her of that.

If any man ever attacked her—or, God forbid, tried to kill her—he would kill him. That was just a fact. He wouldn't be faulted for it. No husband would be. You protected your wife no matter what. And in his own way, he loved her, and he had kept her safe. He had never asked much of her in bed, and he'd spent his life being the ideal husband and father. She accepted him for the man he was, and she didn't ask him to be someone he wasn't.

And what she didn't know didn't hurt her.

"Call me when you get in," he had said as she was pulling out of the driveway.

She would get up there before dark. The kids would benefit from a change in scenery, and he would benefit by being alone for a couple days.

He had stalked Dana Marshall for weeks and had watched her teach her evening class at the Y. She also taught one at the West Side Y. She worked part-time at a shelter for abused women too—she was some kind of social worker or counselor there. He needed to eliminate her because he couldn't have her out there teaching women all over town how to fight back. Having to come up with a plan so quickly again had been challenging. Once he figured it out, the demons hadn't let him rest until he carried it out.

He told his wife that he had to go to the office that night, something he didn't do often, but it happened. Dana—he got her name from envelopes he found in her mailbox—lived in Bonneville, which was a short drive to the south. When he got to her neighborhood, he cased it. He parked a couple streets over and got into her home with no problem. She wasn't married and didn't have a live-in partner. And he had made sure she wasn't expecting anyone that night. He had to surprise her—he couldn't just knock on the door and talk his way in like he'd done many times before. Obviously, that wouldn't work on a woman who taught others to be more aware of their surroundings and to be hyperalert and know how to fend off attackers. He'd known that ambushing her wouldn't be easy but was confident he could do it.

He broke in before she arrived. He had picked up some chloroform because he knew he would need it. Even though she knew how to fight, how to ward him off, and even how to hurt him, she was small. And what she and no one else knew was that he knew martial arts. He practiced his moves when he was alone in the shed. And he wouldn't hesitate to use them.

From his hiding place, he watched her lock the door and turn on her stereo. So much for "situational awareness," one of the phrases on the bulletin board at the Y advertising her class. Tonight, she thought she was safe in her own home. He crept up on her from behind, put his pistol to her neck, and covered her mouth and nose with a chloroform-soaked handkerchief. She jerked into action, but he locked his arms around her torso and held her while the gas did its work. For all her training, she was really much weaker than he'd thought she would be. But men were bigger and stronger than women, even women who were in top shape.

When she passed out, he got busy. He taped her mouth shut and tied her to the bed rails. He started in, and when she came to, he hit her. Hard. Then he continued the work the demons had commanded.

Torture. Violate. Strangle to death.

And he hadn't left any evidence behind.

As usual, he didn't feel any remorse. He didn't really know the meaning of that word. When he completed a mission, after the adrenaline rush subsided, he felt nothing but relief and fulfillment.

In his daily life, he could act modest and humble when necessary, but in truth, he had no humility. He didn't have what other people called low self-esteem. He never got depressed either. That had served him quite well in the military. Unlike some other soldiers he'd known, he hadn't been prone to suicidal feelings. He couldn't imagine how anyone would want to end his own life, no matter how bad things were. At church they said suicide was a permanent solution to a temporary problem. By contrast, his missions were temporary solutions to a permanent problem. And a long time ago, he'd decided that continuing to live his life the way he did was worth taking many, many other lives.

He knew that his problem, if you could call it that, was here to stay. However, one of his gifts was the ability to compartmentalize. He pitied people who couldn't do that. Every time he finished a mission, he put the memory of it into a mental box, locked it, and threw away the key.

If he was going to be honest, he would say that his greatest talent wasn't compartmentalizing or even his ability to blend into the background. Nor was it his photographic memory, his intelligence, or his survival skills in the woods. It wasn't his ability to torture, strangle, and extinguish life without contrition.

It was his gift for telling lies and keeping secrets. His biggest secrets were locked inside the wooden box that he kept in his shed. In it, he stored his journal and souvenirs of his missions, and he guarded the key. Having a shed was very Midwestern and very common. It was the ultimate man cave, and he had his organized just the way he wanted it.

Back in high school, when he kept his wooden box under his bed, he had studied history and drama. He had even acted in a few plays back then. But although he'd wanted to shine when he was on stage, he really didn't want to be the center of attention when he was out in public. He wanted to blend into the background. To remain undiscovered and to continue operating under the radar.

The paradox was that he did need *some* attention. He wanted to win but on his terms, and he wanted credit for what he'd done. He didn't want to be arrested and go to jail. But he felt driven to let the authorities know that the Barbie Killer was back and that they wouldn't be able to find him.

He wanted to taunt them.

After the mission in the hotel, he had deliberated about whether he should contact the police or the press. He'd sent typewritten notes to the police department before, but nothing ever happened. Evidently, they didn't share them with the news media. He wondered if they did share them with the FBI and couldn't really imagine that they had not. The idea of them keeping him out of the local paper while working on his cases with the feds was insupportable.

So this time he had decided to contact the media directly. He was ambidextrous, but since he used his right hand more often, he used his left to write his note and changed his handwriting. He addressed the envelope using the manual typewriter that he kept in his shed. In the days after his note was published, he felt a mixture of pleasure and disappointment. Reading his words on the front page of *The Huntington Post* stroked his ego and gave him a thrill. The Barbie Killer was famous, at least in this town.

He felt oddly let down at the same time. They'd published it without speculating much about him or saying much about the crime. Plus, he knew they wouldn't respond to his message or do what he wanted, which was to get him in the national news. That was something he had craved all these years, and his desire for it had grown stronger with each completed mission. Yet they withheld it from him.

And they wouldn't stop all the whispers.

Chapter 28

After the killer's last two victims—both with ties to Dolly—were found dead, Tim felt like he and Dolly were living in a horror movie that was unfolding in real time. He was convinced that the police weren't going to catch the killer now. After all, they'd had many years to do it, and they hadn't been able to. Had they missed gathering crucial evidence, botched all the crime scenes, or both? Had they ever offered a reward for information about him?

For that matter, why hadn't Peter Hark stepped in at some point and done that? Perhaps it was because he didn't want to attract the attention of the national media. Maybe Hark Industries had been hiding information about the killer all this time in an effort to avoid bad publicity for the company—and for Huntington.

It wasn't inconceivable. The CEO of Hark Industries had a vested interest in keeping the Barbie Killer's existence a secret so as not to scare away potential hires. What if Peter Hark was using his money and power to do that? When the police suspected Roger, top management at Hark had immediately shifted into crisis mode. They'd kept mum about the serial killer's existence for decades only to face the possibility that he could be one of their own. If he were a Hark executive—and a corporate lawyer, at that—it would have been a public relations disaster, not to mention a Human Resources one. How would the company have been able to recruit talented employees and to convince them to move to Huntington?

But now that Roger had been cleared, no one talked about him at work or discussed Maggie Burns' murder anymore. Instead, Dana Marshall—and the fact that the Barbie Killer was still on the loose—were the topics *du jour* among the secretaries and other employees. But many of Tim's colleagues, male and female, shied away from conversations about the killer. Everyone had work to do, and the department was down one very talented lawyer. Roger was currently taking some personal days, and no one knew when—or if—he would be back.

———●———

On Monday, Lynn called Dolly and asked if she wanted to go to lunch the next day. They met at a diner near downtown.

"Well, I'm in shock about Dana," Lynn said after they sat down in a booth.

"I am too. Especially since she must have fought back."

"I know, right? I'm more afraid of him now than ever," Lynn said and gave a little shake of her head.

The waitress appeared, took their orders, and then scurried off.

"Lynn," Dolly said in a low tone, "when I was doing research about the Barbie Killer at the library, I also read about the murder of Denise Hutchins back in the sixties."

"Why?"

"Well, when I first moved here, I heard her family lived in a house that used to be on the lot that we bought and built our house on and that she was murdered in that house."

Lynn's eyes widened. "Oh my gosh. I didn't realize that's where she lived, but I knew it was in that area. I was in junior high when that happened, so I vaguely remember it."

"Yeah, it was a long time ago," Dolly said. "But since her killer was never found, I wonder if she could have been the Barbie Killer's first victim."

Lynn sucked in a breath and opened her eyes wide. "People said her boyfriend did it."

"Randy Hoffman," Dolly said. "The newspaper reported that he was the prime suspect. But the police couldn't find him."

"Right. He disappeared after she was killed, I remember. His parents claimed that he ran away from home."

"Did they file a missing person report or look for him?"

"I don't know—they may have tried to find him. But back then, teenage boys did things like leave home and hitchhike across the country or something. Warren's stepbrother, Ned, left town right after the murder. He had just gotten his draft notice for Vietnam. Warren thinks he went to Canada to avoid having to fight."

The waitress appeared and set their lunch plates on the table. After she left, Lynn continued, "Anyway, a few years later, Warren's parents died in a car wreck. He looked for Ned then, but they never really got along, so he gave up and never tried again. Warren later served in the military, so there's that too."

Dolly asked, "Do you and Warren ever talk about Ned—or about that murder?"

"No," Lynn said emphatically. "I've asked him, and he won't talk about either. I learned a long time ago that he gets upset if he has to re-live the past. It's just too painful for him. His parents were really good people, and I think losing them at a young age forced him to grow up fast. He's been on his own ever since."

"That's rough."

"Yeah," Lynn said. "Anyway, people have been speculating about that murder—and about what happened to Randy—ever since. All anyone knows is that whoever killed Denise slashed her throat. The Barbie Killer strangles his victims, though. Maybe I've seen too many detective shows, but those are two different MO's."

"Good point," Dolly said. "I hadn't thought of that."

On the way home, she wondered why she hadn't. It was possible that the boy who became the Barbie Killer cut his first victim's throat and killed the later ones very differently after torturing them. But it didn't seem likely. The teenage girl's murder could well have been committed in a fit of rage, whether by her boyfriend or someone else. But serial killers had MO's—and they usually left signatures, like a photo of a Barbie doll next to a dead body.

It was time to stop overthinking the cold case and time to start focusing on the real-life murderer. She needed to learn about how he did what he did, what motivated him to do it that way, and why. She would start by going back to the library and studying the criminal psychology of serial killers.

Everyone else could sit back and pretend that they weren't in danger, but she wasn't going to. She couldn't afford to. This was the way forward for her—the only way—and from now on, she needed to be prepared, not scared. And she needed to carry the gun in her purse.

Chapter 29

One evening, Tim and Max went out for a drink after work at a favorite watering hole.

"Have you heard from Roger?" Tim asked as they sat down at a table in the back. After he had taken his personal days off, Roger returned to work and had promptly been fired.

Max nodded. "He's not doing very well."

"I'm going to miss him," Tim confessed, picking up his beer. "I hope he finds something quickly."

"So do I." Max took a sip of his Manhattan. "I can't help but feel sorry for him even though he cheated on his wife. First, he's wrongly accused of killing his girlfriend, then he loses his family, and now, Hark throws him under the bus."

"Do you know why they let him go?"

Max shook his head. "You know as well as I do, upper management can do what they like. They can get rid of any of us, anytime. I guess a murder accusation wasn't a very good look for the company."

Tim knew Max was right about their job security. He'd seen other employees get fired for a lot less. At the last company he worked for, a colleague was told that his suits weren't expensive enough and that his socks weren't long enough to avoid showing bare skin when he crossed his legs. Tim had paid more attention to his attire at work ever since. Another time, he'd heard that a junior employee was canned because he parted his hair on the wrong side. It sounded ridiculous, but it had turned out to be true.

At times, he felt like he was still being evaluated and had better measure up. But during his time with Hark, Tim had built solid relationships with valuable clients and had brought in millions in fee payments. Yet he knew that he was expendable, in spite of the results he'd achieved and his contributions to the bottom line. If Joe wanted to, he could fire Tim for any reason and replace him within a week.

"Meanwhile, the killer's still out there, and the cops *still* don't have a clue," Tim said.

"It does defy understanding, right? But the police must have *something*," Max said. "I don't know. Maybe they have some brilliant strategy that no one knows about and it's helping them get a lot closer to identifying him and picking him up."

"You'd think so. Maybe they're working with the FBI. If they're not, they ought to be," Tim said. "And you know what they say about criminals. Eventually, they make a mistake."

"Yeah, well, I hope he makes his mistake soon and without killing anyone else in the process."

Tim took another sip of his beer. Roger wasn't the killer, but someone else at Hark could be. A couple thousand men worked at headquarters, and a good many of them had lived in Huntington all their lives. But the killer might live somewhere else in Kansas or even in a neighboring state and travel here only to stalk his victims and commit his murders. That could explain the gaps in his killings over the years.

As Tim watched Max order another round, a chill went up his spine.

What if it's Max? He'd lived in Kansas City for decades before working at Hark, but he was very familiar with Huntington. He had sung its praises before Tim moved here. Max didn't have any family in town, so why *did* he know so much about it? Kansas City was a three-hour drive. Had Max lived a double life there and occasionally come down here to torture and strangle women whenever he had an urge?

Tim's mind raced as he considered the possibility. Max had told him lots of things that he'd "heard" about Roger—and about the murder of Maggie Burns—from sources that he never named. Friends and acquaintances. His "buddy" at the police department. And Max was the first person at the office who knew things. Moments ago, he'd seemed furious that the killer was still at large.

Is it all an act? Is Max *the killer hiding in plain sight?*

Tim chased away the thought and told himself to be rational. Yes, there was a slim chance that Max was the Barbie Killer. It was about as likely as if Joe Walton were the killer—or any other man Tim knew or didn't know at Hark. The killer could be a company executive, a blue-collar worker at another company, or a recluse hiding in the woods. He could be an architect, an engineer, or a banker. He could even be Peter Hark, whose reputation for being reserved, thoughtful, and quite intelligent was well known.

Tim couldn't get that idea out of his head as he drove home that night. The killer must have a lot of time to himself. He certainly could be a powerful and successful man and might have a boatload of money that he could use to buy off the police. The sheriff could be on Peter Hark's personal payroll. The police department might have been burying leads about the Barbie Killer all this time while downplaying him to the media and residents—because Peter Hark wanted them to.

Company culture had always seemed odd, but now, it was starting to feel sinister.

Chapter 30

Dolly and Tim had been to the shooting range several times, and she had learned how to safely handle their handgun and how to use it. They kept it in a drawer in Tim's nightstand at night. During the day, Dolly stashed it in her purse, which she kept with her at all times, including when she was at home. Unlike some other women, she carried a lot of things inside it and took it with her everywhere. And no one in the family—even Tim—was allowed to open it.

Before studying the background, behaviors, and motivations of serial killers, Dolly wanted to learn more about this one's past victims than what she had discovered at the library. The press had reported that Dana Marshall was single and lived alone, that she didn't have a boyfriend, and that she had no family in the area. She and all the other victims except for Maggie Burns were killed in their homes, and some were married and had children. The newspaper articles had listed their street addresses, so Dolly decided to drive to each home, meet the people who lived there, and ask if they knew what happened to the victims' families.

Each house was located within twelve miles of the Garners' home. Most were within six miles, and the closest was one mile away in an older neighborhood. Dolly had never been to some of the streets. But two of the houses were on Thirteenth Street, the east-west road that the kids' school was on. Dolly had probably driven right by them hundreds of times.

Their families had lived through the unthinkable. What had become of them? Did they or any of their family members live in those houses now? Did someone else live in them? Or had the homes been torn down and others built there? But Dolly didn't want to just ask the

131

current residents some questions. She wanted to see the homes for her-self—at least the exteriors—because she wanted to visualize the mur-ders in the places where they occurred. She wanted to pick up on the vibes and try to glean clues about the Barbie Killer as a younger man.

It might not be easy to speak to the people who lived in the houses now, but she could try. She could tell them she was a newspaper or mag-azine reporter doing an article about the Barbie Killer. Or she could be honest, say that she wasn't from Huntington, and that she was cu-rious about the killings and the town's history. If they said they didn't know anything about the murders or the victims' families, she could tell them what she knew, which was public record, and then she could gauge their reactions.

⸺◈⸺

It was Dolly's turn to host book club that night. Tim had taken the kids out for pizza and a movie, and Heidi arrived early and before anyone else. They went into the kitchen and set the wine bottles and glasses on the island.

"Everything looks so yummy," Heidi said. Dolly had prepared a few appetizers—fruit and raw veggies with a dip, cheese and crackers, and mini ham sandwiches. "And your kitchen is so clean and tidy!"

"It's where everyone gathers, at least at first," Dolly said, smiling. Heidi and she had been to each other's homes before, but her kitchen *was* spotless right now. "In twenty-four hours, this room will be back to its normal state of clutter and chaos."

"My kitchen is always in a state of chaos, and it's even worse while I'm cooking. Matt is constantly complaining about how I don't clean up as I go and I drop things on the floor. But then he swoops in after-ward and takes care of it."

"Lucky you!" Dolly poured each of them a glass of wine.

They heard the doorbell ring and the door open as Celeste and Susie walked in. Betsy and the others arrived soon after. Everyone did gather in the kitchen and began chatting. No one mentioned the killer or his most recent murder, but Dolly felt like they were dancing around the topic. Finally, when there was a lull in conversation, Betsy brought it up.

"Has anyone heard anything else about Dana?" she asked as she looked around the room.

No one said anything for a moment or two. Then Susie spoke up for everybody. "I haven't, and I'm still freaked out about it."

"Me too," said Betsy, eyeing the group. "I hope the police are doing all they can to find him."

"It's got to be their top priority," Heidi said, glancing at Dolly.

"I'd rather not talk about the Barbie Killer," Celeste said. "Obviously, he's not dead or in jail like people thought." She sniffed. "I think it's just a matter of time until they pick him up."

"I hope you're right," Betsy said. "But I've heard that said more times than I can remember."

There was another awkward pause. Some people exchanged glances, and others trained their eyes on the floor. It was the tensest moment of the night—and of any book club meeting that Dolly had attended.

"Well, Bob says they'll find him soon," Celeste added. "He has a friend in the police department. And before you ask, we are locking our doors and windows now. We'd be crazy not to. Bob's got weapons too."

"So does Rick," said Susie.

Rather than chiming in that her husband—that *they*—did as well, Dolly kept silent. For one crazy second, she considered the possibility that the killer was married to Celeste or Susie.

Ten minutes later, they all sat down in the den and began talking about the book. The novel, called *A Lifelong Love Affair with France*, was a refreshing change from the mysteries and thrillers they'd been reading over the last several months. Dolly had enjoyed them, but now, it felt like they were all living in a true crime novel that nobody wanted to read. The subject of the Barbie Killer didn't come up again that evening.

After everyone left, Dolly turned to Heidi. "I'm think I'm going to do something," she said, "and I want you to tell me what you think of it."

"Okay, shoot."

Dolly described her idea of visiting the prior victims' homes and why she wanted to.

"I think it's a great idea, and I want to go with you," Heidi said. "Why *not* ask them what they know? I mean, what's the downside? Plus, isn't it about time people start talking to each other about the serial killer in this town?"

"What if we meet someone who doesn't know one of his victims died in their house?"

"If they don't, they should," Heidi said. "And we can tell them. Let's go knock on their doors and tell them straight up that we're trying to piece together what happened because we want to know more about the killer and his past. I bet they'll be glad to talk to us about it."

"I hope so, but I guess we'll find out."

Chapter 31

A few days later, while the kids were in school, Dolly and Heidi set out to visit the prior victims' homes. The two that were on Thirteenth Street were older brick ranch houses. There were no cars in the driveways, and nobody answered the door at either, so they looked in through the front windows. Each was vacant. There was no furniture inside or any other indication that someone lived in them. Both had dingy wall-to-wall carpeting and looked as if they had seen better days.

"They could be rentals," Heidi said. "I wonder who owns them or what the deal is."

The third house was a few miles closer to town and on the West Side. It was an old white clapboard house that didn't look as if the owner kept it up. A seventy-something lady with thin gray hair and smoker's wrinkles encircling her lips opened the door and greeted them.

"You're not the first to ask, you know," she said after they introduced themselves and explained why they were there. "By the way, my name's Lois. You both seem nice, so I don't mind telling you about the house. Would you like to come in while we talk? I could make some tea if you like."

Dolly and Heidi exchanged glances, signaling they ought to take Lois up on her offer.

"That would be great," Heidi said. "But no tea for me, thank you."

Dolly seconded that, and Lois ushered them inside and into a small carpeted living area, where the three of them sat down.

"You don't mind if I smoke, do you?" Lois asked.

"Of course not," Dolly said, looking around the room. "How long have you lived here?"

"I bought it fifteen years ago, but I had no clue that one of those murders happened in it. I didn't find out until a year later, and when I did, I was furious."

"That's awful," Heidi said, shaking her head. "I would have been angry too."

"Hmm. The law is that the seller has to disclose something like that," said Dolly.

Lois nodded emphatically. "That's right. But they didn't. I've tried to sell the place, but nobody was interested, and I can't afford to buy another one without selling this one."

"It's not right that you weren't told before you bought it," Heidi said. "Have you thought about suing?"

"Lawyers cost too much money," Lois said. "Money I don't have. So I'm stuck here, I guess." She leaned in closer and lowered her voice. "Between you and me, ever since I found out, I've been afraid the killer would return to the crime scene." She shuddered. "Luckily, he hasn't, and my neighbors are pretty vigilant about watching out for me and each other."

"Do you know what happened to the victim's family?" Dolly asked.

"She was a single woman in her twenties." Lois raised her eyebrows. "But you probably knew that. I heard she had no family here in Huntington. Maybe that was one reason she was on his radar." She threw up her hands. "I'm just speculating, though. Who knows?"

"Do you know anything about the actual murder?" Heidi asked. "Like where it happened and how he got into the house?"

Lois brightened. "Oh, yes. Well, I know the story that's gone around, but I can't swear that it's true. I'll show you the room, if you like." She made a face. "But don't get nervous when you see it. Remember, I live here."

"Of course not," Dolly said. "We're just curious even though it took place so long ago."

Lois stood up. "Follow me, then."

She led them down a short, narrow hallway past a bathroom and showed them into a decent-size room in the back of the house with a closet. A low shelf and an old desk and chair sat in a corner, but otherwise, the room was empty.

"It's a bedroom—or was," Lois said. She puffed her cigarette and then added in a low tone, "It was *her* bedroom. She was found tied to the bed and had been strangled to death. He did other things to her, too, but I don't like to say them out loud. I did hear there was no blood."

Dolly bit her lip. Reading about the murders had been chilling, but now that she was standing in the place where this one happened, the reality of it hit her, and so did the terror.

"Do you know how the killer got into the house?" Heidi asked.

Lois nodded. "I heard that he knocked on her front door, and she let him come in! She didn't know him, though. Probably told her he was having car trouble and asked to use the phone or something like that. Whatever it was, she was naïve, I guess, and too nice. Don't *ever* let a stranger into your house, especially if you're alone." She shook her head. "Poor woman."

They chatted with Lois a little more and learned that this murder had been one of the first, happening back in the 1970s. They thanked her and said goodbye before getting in the car.

"Who's next?" Heidi asked.

The next two addresses led them to vacant lots—or fields, it looked like. They were the most rural, north of town. Evidently, like the house that had once stood on the Garners' property, they had been demolished.

The next address was a corner lot, and the house almost looked like it had been condemned. They parked on the street, and a man in his thirties with a tattoo on his wrist answered the door. He seemed as happy to talk to them as Lois had been.

"I rent," he said. "But I knew about the history before I moved in. I don't know anything about the victim, though. Anyways, according to the landlord, two other people lived here before me and both left because of what happened. I guess they got spooked." He shrugged.

"You didn't, though?" Heidi asked.

"Nah. I mean, what happened happened. Way before my time. The price is right, and it's in a quiet area and near my job. So I'm fine with it. Not sure I'd want to buy it, though."

"I wonder if the owner—your landlord—knows what happened to the people who lived here when the murder happened," Dolly said. The victim in this house had been married. "Or anything about the murder itself."

"No idea. He's only owned it for a few years, so I'd guess he doesn't." He looked at his watch. "If that's all you wanted, I've got to go, so…"

"Sure," Heidi said. "Thanks for your time."

"I'm not upset that he didn't invite us in," Dolly said when they climbed into the car again. "I didn't need to see the inside to get a feel for the place."

"Me neither," said Heidi. "It felt like either he didn't know where the woman was killed in there, or he didn't want to talk about it."

There were three more houses to check, and two of them were vacant. All three were replicas of the two houses on Thirteenth Street. The final one was only a mile from Dolly's house.

"I was horrified when I found out," the resident, whose name was Shirley, said. She had an apron on and looked like a housewife. They could hear a television blaring somewhere inside and kids babbling. "Honestly, when we bought it a few years ago, we knew that a woman was attacked in it. But we didn't know she'd been stalked and murdered by the Barbie Killer."

"I wonder why no one told you," Heidi said, glancing at Dolly. "Legally, they have to disclose a murder being committed in the house to a buyer."

"If they did, we missed it," Shirley said. "But the real estate agent should have made sure we knew. I want to sell the house and move, but Bill says we can't—not yet anyway." She looked behind her, presumably in the direction of the kids as if to make sure they weren't listening. Then she leaned toward Dolly and Heidi and said quietly, "If you want to know the truth, I think this house is haunted. Not that I would tell *that* to a potential buyer, mind. But weird stuff happens, you know? Like sometimes I hear things, or I feel someone's presence. But when I do, there's nobody there." Her eyes were wide.

Dolly felt her knees begin to shake. "Do you know anything about the victim's family or where they went?"

"No, sorry," Shirley said. "All I really know is that her husband sold it to the people we bought it from. Don't know how he managed to do that, though. I guess he didn't tell *them* about the murder either."

Since there were children in the house, Dolly felt it would be awkward to ask Shirley if they could come in. "Thanks so much for talking with us," she said. "If we find out anything about it, or about the family, do you want us to come back and let you know?"

"No, I don't think so," Shirley said. "I mean, I hope they're okay and all. But I think the less I know, the better, you know?"

"Well, I'm a little creeped out," Heidi said a few moments later when they got in the car. "But not as much as I would be if I lived in one of these houses."

"Same here," Dolly said. "What do you think about Shirley telling us she hears noises or feels like someone is there?"

Heidi pressed her lips together and then said, "Well, if it isn't haunted, then maybe somebody is watching her." She looked at Dolly. "I think it's very odd that she and that other lady weren't told about the murders when they bought their houses."

"It isn't just odd, it's illegal," Dolly said. "There must be some kind of loophole, or maybe it was in the fine print and they didn't see it. If I were one of them, I'd be pissed."

"The realtors had to know. They just hid the truth."

"Like lots of people do in this town," Dolly said, "and have been doing for a long time."

———●———

"You did *what*?" Tim asked Dolly while he and Dolly had a drink that night. "And why?"

"I told you I wanted to learn more about the past murders," she said matter-of-factly.

"Yeah, but you didn't say you and Heidi planned to go around knocking on doors and asking strangers about the victims." *What if the killer was watching them and gets angry?*

She tossed her head. "I just wanted to see what I could find out from them. And there's no harm in asking people questions. Only a few people were at home anyway, and they didn't seem to mind talking to us. Nobody knew anything, though."

"So it was a dead end then."

"Kind of. I didn't think I'd learn that much information, but I wanted to see for myself where the murders happened. Two of the houses were gone—they must have been torn down—and four were vacant. One guy we spoke to, who was a renter, knew about the murder in his house. But two other people we talked to said they didn't know about them before they bought their homes, and they were upset when they found out."

"I bet they were," Tim said. "If you decide to go back to any of them, tell me, okay?"

"I'm not planning to, but if I change my mind, I will."

"Good. Now, I've got something to tell you that I think you'll be very happy to hear." He cleared his throat. "I've talked to three executive recruiters recently about getting a new job somewhere else. They'll be in touch about positions in other cities that might be a good fit and will set up interviews for me. I've also contacted some former colleagues and business associates and let them know that I'm looking."

"That's great, Tim!"

"The thing is, I don't know how long it will take to find a new position," he cautioned. "I could get lucky and get an offer soon, though. If working for Hark for less than two years is a negative to a future employer, so be it. I hope I find a job that pays as much as this one, but if I have to take a pay cut—or if we have to take a loss on this house or both—that's fine with me. We're in a good spot financially now. We can do it, and we'll survive."

"I agree," Dolly said emphatically. "And wherever we go, I can get a job if I need to."

"Let's talk about that when we know more. You don't mind uprooting the kids and starting all over again?"

"Not at all," she said. She would do it in a heartbeat. "They'll adjust, and we'll be fine. We'll make it work, no matter what."

Chapter 32

The following day, Dolly went back to the library to read anything she could find about serial killers. She found a lot of material that had been written about them, but nothing that delved into their psyches. Instead, it was all facts describing what they'd done, where they'd done it, and when and how. Each one was unique and had his own modus operandi—MO. All of them were men—at least, all the ones Dolly read about were. And all were, by definition, evil.

Then she discovered articles describing interviews of the killers conducted by criminal psychologists. Not surprisingly, most were cryptic in their responses, displayed no empathy for others, and were remorseless about their crimes. Some claimed they were driven to do what they did, as if it were out of their control, and that there was no rhyme or reason to their choice of victims. A few said that if they hadn't been caught, they would have kept on killing. The more she read, the more Dolly was convinced they were mentally ill. And it was said that crazy people had a lot of energy, especially when they were young.

None of what she'd learned so far was going to help her protect herself from the Barbie Killer, though. Rather than study other killers, she needed to focus on him and his behavior. She needed insight into his motivations and methods, and she needed to examine his pattern of killing over time.

After three hours of research, it was time to leave and go pick up the kids at school. She'd made some progress, at least. Now, she knew more about serial killers in general, and was starting to focus on the one who lived in this town. She hurried out to her car, unlocked it, and opened her door. Then she saw a yellow folded note sitting on the driver's seat.

She shut the door and quickly looked around the parking lot. No one was around, and there were only a few other parked cars. She reached into her bag and placed her right hand on her weapon. With the other hand, she opened the sliding door behind her seat. Nobody was there.

Her heart pounding, she searched the van's interior. It was empty. She shut the sliding door, snatched the note from the driver's seat, jumped in, and locked the car. Breathe, she told herself. Then she opened the note.

You won't know when I'm coming. It won't be much longer.

Under the message was a pencil drawing of a nude woman with the impossible figure of a Barbie doll. She had a rope pulled around her neck, and her eyes and mouth were wide open.

Dolly was shaking. She had to calm down, however, so she could get to the school and get home with the kids. Whoever had left the note had unlocked her car, put the note in her seat, and then locked it. Unless... Had she forgotten to lock her doors when she got here?

That had to be it. If she had locked her car, he would have left the note on her windshield like he had before. And it had to be the same person because it was on a yellow piece of paper again and had been typed on a typewriter.

The drawing was chilling. This had to be from the Barbie Killer. If it was, why was he targeting her? *Was* it because she was Maggie's looka-like? Or... was it because of where she lived? Had she been right all along about their house having bad karma and that one day they would have to pay?

There was a chance that the note hadn't been left by him but by a copycat trying to scare her. Whoever it was, he'd succeeded. But she wasn't going to give in to fear, and she wasn't going to let him win. Her panic subsided somewhat and began to be replaced by determination as she drove to St. Thomas More school. She would call Tim and then the police when she got home. Minutes later, the kids were in the car, and they were on the way.

As soon as she got them settled and busy doing their homework, she grabbed the cordless phone and stepped outside onto the back patio, closing the glass sliding door behind her.

"*What?*" Tim asked after she read the message to him. "I'm coming home now."

"I'm going to call the police to report it after we hang up."

"Good. Tell them about the first note too."

It didn't take long for her to reach someone at the department, but after she recounted what had happened, the officer's reaction was lukewarm.

"I know this was very disturbing, and you did the right thing by letting us know," he told her. "That said, this isn't a crime."

"It's harassment, isn't it?"

"It may well be, but unless you saw who did it, or someone else did, there's not much we can do."

Dolly was incredulous. "But after the recent murders, aren't you looking for anything at all that would lead you to the killer? Such as threatening notes like these?"

"Of course we are. Not sure I'd call those threats, though. Fact is, there are a lot of nutcases out there, ma'am."

Frustrated, Dolly let out a sigh. This was why she hadn't bothered to call the cops earlier. "What am I supposed to do, then?"

"Stay alert, and call us back if the situation escalates."

Dolly hung up, walked back inside, and put the phone on the kitchen counter. While she waited for Tim to walk in the door, she picked up the notes she had taken at the library.

Then she realized something. The Barbie Killer seemed to be doing a few things differently now than he had in the past. His MO was the same, but he had changed his pattern of killing. Before the Garners moved to Huntington, he had killed his victims at random, stalking them and seizing his opportunity, apparently without putting himself in danger of detection. He didn't write and leave threatening notes to let them know he was watching them.

He hadn't been able to stalk Maggie because she didn't live here in town, but he probably did stalk Dana. But did he *deliberately* choose to kill both of them for some warped reason, rather than at random or on a whim? Since he killed Maggie in her hotel room, he had exposed himself and risked being seen. And although he killed Dana in her home, he likely knew she was skilled at self-defense. He must have thought that he was more adept than her and much stronger and didn't mind taking a gamble.

Maybe he had mellowed, now that he was older. Maybe he was getting tired and had become less risk averse because he just didn't care anymore. Perhaps, deep down, he *wanted* to be captured. Or it could be that he had gotten cocky with age and sincerely believed he was invincible and would always get away with his horrific crimes. From time to time, he had indicated that he wanted attention. That was something else that hadn't changed.

Maybe he had always had a complete lack of humility and a huge ego, both of which made him blind to the fact that he was only one mistake away from getting caught.

Chapter 33

On the first Saturday of May, Tim and Dolly took the kids to the Riverfest.

They loaded them into the van, headed downtown, and parked on a side street. Throngs of people were coming out of the woodwork from every direction and making their way toward the festival. Lots of uniformed police officers were on duty, and Dolly felt safer there than she had in weeks. Several city blocks had been closed, and there was a lot to see and do. Dolly took Audrey's hand while Tim and the boys bought rolls of tickets for the rides. Food trucks and stands sold carnival fare like corn dogs, turkey legs, and funnel cakes. The scents coming from deep fryers swirled in the air, along with a pungent mixture of grime and sweat.

Dolly glanced around, taking everything in. The Riverfest was clearly and unapologetically American and distinctively Midwestern. It was a cross between *Oklahoma!* and *The Music Man,* mixed with a quarter cup of *Pollyanna* and a half cup of *The Wizard of Oz.* She almost thought Dorothy and Toto were around the corner, the Wicked Witch on their heels.

The boys took off for the rides with Tim. Audrey and Dolly looked around for activities more Audrey's speed, of which there were several. She squeezed her mom's hand and looked up at her.

"Can I have a snow cone, Mommy?"

Dolly deliberated for a second. They wouldn't eat lunch for a while, but it was very hot. A cup of shaved ice seeped in flavored sugar syrup wouldn't hurt, Dolly decided, and would spike her energy and help her stay hydrated. And Cole and Hugh weren't here to gripe about Audrey always getting what she wanted.

"Sure, sweetie."

They walked over to a stand, and Audrey decided on a flavor. Then, all of a sudden, Dolly had a feeling that someone was staring at her. She turned and locked eyes with him.

He was accompanied by a woman and two young kids. He looked rather familiar, but Dolly couldn't place him. Was he a neighbor or someone from school or church? Why was he looking at her?

She turned her attention back to Audrey, paid for the snow cone, and grabbed her hand. She looked over at the man again to make sure that he wasn't still looking at her. He was. Then he nodded at her and faded into the crowd.

A minute later, it hit her. It was Gary, the window repairman. The *creepy* window repairman who had stared at her chest that day and made her feel uncomfortable. She bristled.

Is Gary the guy who wrote the creepy notes? Is he the Barbie Killer?

It was possible. But it was also quite possible that he was just an odd guy and his nod was a friendly gesture because he'd recognized her. In any case, she wasn't going to freak out.

Audrey pulled on her hand and gave her a pleading look, bringing her back to the present. Audrey was struggling with her melting snow cone, trying to keep it contained in its flimsy cup. Dolly came to the rescue and helped her fix it, and they wandered on and then found Tim and the boys. She kept an eye out for neighbors but didn't see any. She didn't see anybody from Hark either. There were lots of people with tattoos and body piercings, wearing cut-off jean shorts, faded T-shirts, and skimpy halter tops—the riffraff, according to Roger. But that was normal for a carnival like this on a hot day, and who cared anyway?

A little later, the five of them ate lunch, and Tim and Dolly had a beer. Then they bumped into Heidi, Matt, and their crew. They chatted for a few minutes and decided to meet by the river to eat dinner and watch the fireworks together that evening.

"You think the kids will make it that long?" Dolly asked Tim quietly after the Barrons went on their way.

He shrugged. "We could go home, give them a break, and come back for dinner. Or not."

The boys overheard him and flashed looks of incredulity at both him and Dolly.

"I don't want to go home!" Cole cried.

"I want to stay *all day* and see the fireworks tonight," Hugh added. "You *said* we could."

That was the ultimate punch, their parental Achilles' heel, and the boys knew it. Tim and Dolly were very big on doing what they promised—doing what they said they would do.

Especially Dolly.

She lowered her chin and looked at Hugh. "If you really want to, fine, we will." Then she shot Cole and Audrey warning looks. "But don't whine and complain when you get tired later on. If you do, we *will* go home and we won't come back."

"We won't whine!" Audrey said. "Promise!"

"Okay, we'll stay. Decision made," said Tim, satisfied and ready to change the subject.

Dolly thought the boys would be fine and could power through and hang out all day. Audrey might have trouble. Hopefully she'd get a second wind and wouldn't end up exhausted.

The guys found arcade games nearby and started playing. Audrey didn't want to join them.

She tugged Dolly's arm. "Can I get my face painted, Mommy?"

There was an artist a few feet away, and several little girls were standing in line.

"Sure, honey."

They joined the queue, and a few seconds later, Lynn and her daughter, Bridget, walked up behind them. Mother and daughter were wearing shorts and T-shirts.

"Hey, Dolly," Lynn said, smiling. "Having fun?"

"Hi, Lynn! Yes. Are your husband and son here too?"

"They're over at the arcade, I think." She looked at the girls, who had hugged each other and were holding hands. "I hope the face paint doesn't smear on their little faces in this heat!"

"Tim has our boys over there too," Dolly said. "It *is* pretty hot today."

"And no breeze. The one day you *want* the wind to blow, and it doesn't!" Lynn said.

It was Audrey's turn, and the face-painting lady greeted her. "Hi, honey! Do you know what you want?"

Audrey sat down in the chair and bounced in it. "Sunflowers!" She pointed to her cheeks.

"Good choice, sweetie. That's the Kansas state flower! Now, sit still for a few minutes, okay?"

Dolly smiled and hovered nearby as the lady took her delicate brush to Audrey's face. After they had moved into the house, their real estate agent had given her a pewter serving dish shaped like a sunflower as a thank-you gift. When Audrey's and Bridget's cheeks were properly decorated, the girls and their moms strolled around, the moms letting them decide where to stop and what to do.

Half an hour later, Lynn's husband and son appeared. "There you are!" Lynn said. She put her hand on her son's shoulder. He was about Cole's age. "Dolly, this is Paul."

"Nice to meet you," Dolly said then turned to Warren. "Having a good time?"

"You bet," he said. "We come to the Riverfest every year. The kids love it." He looked at Lynn. "Are you and Bridget ready to eat lunch?"

"Yeah," Lynn said and turned toward Dolly. "See you later. Have a fun rest of your day!"

They said goodbye, and Dolly and Audrey headed toward the amusement rides to look for Tim and the boys.

"Mom!" Cole exclaimed when he spied Dolly several minutes later. He ran up to her and Audrey. "The roller coaster is awesome! We've ridden it five times!"

Dolly ruffled his hair, glad he was still young enough to let her. "Sounds like a record!"

Tim and Hugh walked up, and Tim asked how Audrey was holding out.

"Just fine," Dolly said. "We've been pacing ourselves. If you want a break from the action, we can switch. Or we could stay together and play it by ear."

"I don't need a break, but let's do stick together." He looked at Audrey. "Those are pretty flowers, sweetie."

Audrey reached for his hand and beamed at him. "Thanks, Daddy."

"We ran into Lynn and her daughter and hung out for a while," Dolly said to him, "and then her son and husband showed up, and I got to meet them."

As they wandered, Cole told his mom everything he and Tim and Hugh had done in detail. Hugh walked quietly a few feet behind them, his eyes darting around as he looked for kids he knew. Dolly didn't see any of the Gradys or Gary again. That evening, when they joined the Barron family for dinner, all five Garners were tired but happy, and Cole and Audrey fell asleep on the way home.

Chapter 34

The end of the school year was getting closer, and the kids' extracurricular activities were winding down. Hugh was busy studying for finals and for a big oral exam, but his brother and sister had little homework and more free time to play after school.

One weekday afternoon near the end of May, Cole burst into the kitchen through the sliding glass door and found his mother folding laundry in the den.

"Mom! Audrey's gone!" He panted, his face red.

Panic arose in Dolly's throat. "What?"

"She's gone. I can't find her."

"I thought you were watching her!"

"I was, but she disappeared."

She grabbed him. "Where were you when you last saw her?"

"We were playing in the Secret Place."

"What's the 'Secret Place?'"

"That's what we call it. It's just a place we play. It's across from the park."

She pulled him toward the garage. "Show me."

They jumped into the van, and Dolly's heart raced as she imagined the worst. What if someone had grabbed Audrey?

"Turn here," he said, pointing left.

Keeping her eyes peeled, Dolly turned onto the subdivision's main drag, its busiest avenue used by almost all residents.

"You said the park."

"No. Near the park. Down there." He pointed again.

The park was about a half mile from home and in the center of Glenlake. There was a large playground in it, a pool, and a baseball field. All year, the kids had told Dolly that was where they went if they weren't nearby. They had never mentioned the "Secret Place."

"Here it is," said Cole.

She slowed down and stopped the car next to a few trees and bushes. They jumped out and began calling out Audrey's name.

Dolly was frantic. Her heart was pounding almost out of her chest. She was more of a free-rein mom than some, but Audrey was much too young to be wandering around alone, and she never should have put Cole in charge of his sister. Anything could have happened to her.

"How long ago did you see her?" It had taken less than five minutes to get here, but it probably took him longer than that to get home once he'd realized she was gone. And who knew how long it had been before he noticed?

"I don't know."

"You stay in this area—the Secret Place? I'll drive around and look for her. I'll come back and get you."

She hopped back behind the wheel, praying that Audrey was down the street and safe.

Her heart still pounding, she called out her daughter's name as she drove slowly through the neighborhood, her face flushed and tears welling in her eyes. After she covered half the subdivision, she headed back to the Secret Place and saw Cole waving his arms.

"She's over there! On the swings!"

Dolly yanked her head around and saw her in the distance. *Thank God.* The park was across this street, and the playground was on the far side of it.

"Come on!"

He got in the car. Seconds later, they pulled into the small parking lot.

"Audrey!" Dolly called as she ran toward her. Cole followed.

"Hi, Mommy," she said, looking surprised and sheepish.

Dolly squatted down and wrapped Audrey in her arms.

"What's the matter, Mommy?" she asked, bewildered.

"You didn't stay with Cole, honey," Dolly said softly. A tear trickled down her cheek. Her heart rate had slowed, but her face was still red.

"I got bored," she said, looking at her brother. "I told him I was going to the playground."

"Well, he didn't hear you. But you shouldn't have come here without him, sweetie. You're supposed to stay together. We're going home now." Dolly stood up, held Audrey's hand, and started walking toward the car.

Audrey gave her a pleading look. "Can't I stay here and play?"

"Another time. But not by yourself."

"I wasn't by myself, Mommy," Audrey said.

"There's nobody else here," Cole said, lifting his palms and his shoulders in an exaggerated motion.

"There was! There was a man on the bench over there." She pointed to her left, and Dolly whipped her head around, scanning their surroundings. No one was on the bench or anywhere else.

"Who and when?" Dolly asked, tightening her grip on Audrey's hand.

"I dunno. A dad, I guess," she said. "I saw him sitting there when I got here, but I didn't see his kids. I guess they were playing somewhere else."

Alarm bells rang in Dolly's head. *What's a man doing sitting on a bench here by himself?*

"Have you ever seen him before?"

Audrey shook her head.

"Did he say anything to you?"

"No, he just watched me. He left right before you got here. I'm sorry, Mommy."

That night, Dolly told Tim what had happened while they thought all three kids were watching TV in the basement. But Cole had crept up the stairs and was listening to his parents' conversation.

Finally, he poked his head around the corner.

"Tell me about the Secret Place, son," Tim said.

Cole crouched as he walked in, a worried expression on his face. "Am I in trouble, Dad?"

"No. You did the right thing coming to get Mom. Why do you call it the Secret Place?"

He shrugged. "I dunno. We just do. Because no one else plays there, I guess."

"Is that why you like to go there? Because it's someplace no one else goes?" Dolly asked.

Cole nodded slowly. "And because it's not the park. I mean, the park's fun, but the Secret Place is more fun."

"Where is it?" Tim asked Dolly.

"Next to a sidewalk," she said, "in a shady area under some trees. In the common area between someone's back fence and the street."

Tim looked back at Cole. "Here's the deal. Mom and I have decided that Audrey can't go off to play anywhere without an adult anymore. She won't be tagging along after you guys, and you won't have to watch her."

"But she *likes* the Secret Place. Me and her have fun playing there."

Dolly and Tim exchanged glances. Cole rarely admitted that he liked to play with Audrey.

"Even so, she can't go there with you anymore," Tim said. "You can still go there with Hugh, or your friends, or by yourself. But be careful crossing the street."

"I will, Dad. Can I go now?"

He and Dolly nodded, and Cole scampered back downstairs.

Tim looked at Dolly. "Did she tell you what the man on the bench looked like?"

"No. All she said was that he looked 'normal.'"

"And neither you nor Cole saw him."

"No, he was already gone."

A few moments passed, and then Dolly broke the silence. "If anything had happened to her, I would never have forgiven myself."

Tim shook his head. "Me neither. But kids should be able to play outside in their own neighborhood. We did it every day when we were little."

"Well, they can't anymore. Certainly not here," Dolly said.

"Okay," Tim began. "This was a big scare and a wake-up call for us. And now, we're making the right decision. She can play in our yard, but she can't go anywhere else unless she's with an adult."

"I agree," Dolly said. "She's just not old enough to go play by herself. It's just too risky."

"I wonder if she'll ever be old enough," Tim said.

⎯⎯⎯◉⎯⎯⎯

For Dolly, a man hanging out by himself in the park and watching Audrey wasn't only a wake-up call. It was a call to action.

The person who'd written the notes Dolly had received might very well be the Barbie Killer. Whoever he was, the author had been watching her. Was he watching her daughter too?

There was no way to know, but it was past time to double down. Calling the police hadn't worked, and she suspected that they would be just as unhelpful if she contacted them to report what had happened today and told them about the man loitering by himself at the park. But she had to do something. What she had learned so far about serial killers—and what she speculated about this one—weren't enough. She needed to try to understand them and what went on in their twisted minds. She needed more insight into the Barbie Killer's behavior and MO to come up with theories about him and what drove him.

He had changed his pattern lately—even if only slightly—which might be significant. He could have quirks and idiosyncrasies that had evolved over time. He was human, so he had flaws and weaknesses like everyone else. He might even have a phobia or two. Since he had literally gotten away with murder for decades, perhaps his ego led him to become overconfident and to think he was untouchable.

He must have a vulnerability, an Achilles' heel, and if Dolly kept looking, maybe she would figure out what it was. And if she was lucky, she might be able to use it against him.

Chapter 35

The next day at work, he was busy doing something a little unusual, and it was taking all of his focus to complete. But he didn't mind that kind of thing, and it kept life interesting. He treasured the autonomy and freedom that he had to make decisions and to do his work the way he knew how. As he walked down the hall of the office building, he kept his head down. A manager in a gray suit and a blue tie passed by, barely giving him a nod as he hurried on. He didn't know the man's name and decided that he must be new. Another corporate transplant who probably didn't want to be here.

He found the room he had been searching for and quietly stepped inside. He could get what he needed done in here without being distracted or summoned. The last thing he wanted to do was to get into a conversation with anyone right now.

But people here knew not to bother him. Most of them were Kansans like him, hardworking people who were quiet and reserved. People from out of state weren't like that. They asked too many questions and stirred things up. When outsiders moved here, they affected the local economy, too, driving up home prices and taking jobs away from residents. And they complained about everything—the weather, the wind, the terrain, and even the way people talked. They made it clear they didn't want to live here, yet they came.

He loved living in Kansas, and he loved the prairie. Some people thought it was desolate here, but he felt it was peaceful. He had fond memories of when his son was little and they would go to a nearby field or meadow and fly kites together. Staring at the tallgrass and wild sunflowers gave him the feeling some said they had when they saw the ocean. When he looked at the ocean, though, he didn't feel calm or at peace. The sea was a dangerous place, full of monsters and beasts living a hidden life in darkness. When he really wanted serenity, he would drive up through the Flint Hills in northeastern Kansas. He enjoyed his occasional jaunts alone up there and often over to Kansas City, as well as driving around Huntington.

For obvious reasons, he had never driven back to the houses where his earlier missions had been completed. Until recently.

Well, except for one. From time to time, he had peered inside the house where the married woman with two kids had lived. He had even been inside, late at night, while the man who lived in the house now snored and his wife tossed and turned. He had watched her get up in the middle of the night and walk to the kitchen to get a glass of water. She was very jumpy, and once or twice, he was afraid she saw him in the shadows. He had also spied on her during the day a few times when he had the chance. But ever since that time in the eighties, when he'd heard that baby crying in the nursery after his mission was complete, he'd avoided women with small children because he didn't like leaving kids without a mother.

He had followed Dolly and Heidi at a safe distance while they were driving to the houses that day and watched them talking to some of the residents on their front porches. They even went inside one—the only one he still visited.

Why did they go to those houses, and what were they up to? He often saw the two of them together, walking out of their fitness club to their cars, or going into a restaurant or a shop. But he hadn't overheard them talking and had never suspected that they discussed him. Now, he knew they did. He needed to eliminate both of them. Then maybe the demons would let him rest for a while.

One day after work, he stopped at the toy store to pick up two brunette Barbies. When the cashier rang them up, she gave him a curious look. For a split second, he wondered if she knew who he was and whether she had seen him before.

"You meant to buy two that are exactly alike?" she asked, gazing into his face.

Taken aback, he stammered, "They're for my twin nieces. Got to have everything exactly the same. You know how kids are." Had the toy-store clerks been put on notice to remember any man buying a Barbie doll?

"Uh-huh," the girl murmured, still staring at him. "Hope they don't get them mixed up."

"Oh, they won't." He paid in cash and hurried to the exit.

On the short drive home, he thought about Dolly's little girl. Their neighborhood park had been empty when he got there, and all he'd wanted was some solitude, a short escape from his busy workday. Then that child ran over and jumped on a swing, facing in his direction. She spotted him, as children often did, and locked eyes with him, which made him uncomfortable. She seemed to be studying him as if she knew who he was.

Then the whispers had begun, so he'd gotten up quietly and left.

Chapter 36

The next morning, Tim got up and drove the three miles to work like he did every day. He said hello to the secretaries and operations people on the way to his office. He looked over his agenda and went through his messages and email.

Then he got a call from Joe asking him to come to his office.

"Close the door behind you," Joe said as Tim walked in.

He did so then sat down and waited. His brow was furrowed, and he had a feeling that whatever Joe was going to say was bad news.

Before Joe spoke, he shook his head. "I hate to have to talk to you about this," he said, looking grim.

Tim's ears pricked. *What is this about?*

"However," he continued, "I'll get right to it so we can talk about a solution. A female employee in the department has come to me and complained about you."

Tim was stunned and bewildered. Speechless, he cupped his chin in his hand, covering his mouth, as he racked his brain about his behavior at the office. *Who could have an issue with him and would go to Joe with it?*

"Look, Tim, you're one of the stars here. You do know that, don't you? But all it takes is some woman with a stick up her ass—excuse me, but there it is. She's uptight, to say the least." His brows shot up as he gave Tim a pointed look.

"Who? What did she say?"

He sat back and listened as Joe explained. One of the secretaries—he wouldn't disclose her name—said that Tim had told her she looked nice one day. It didn't matter that he was only trying to be friendly by paying her a compliment and didn't mean anything by it.

She had taken it as a sexual innuendo, according to Joe. She had also overheard Tim say something about Roger when he was in police custody.

"She didn't like it when you said you couldn't believe he cheated on his wife," Joe said.

Tim's jaw dropped. *What the hell?* "So, now I can't have an opinion? Or express it?"

"Not at the office," he said. "Not about something personal anyway. Look, I know lots of people here were talking about that situation. Gossiping about it. I didn't think you were, and I still don't. She didn't say that you were, but she said you made her feel uncomfortable."

"Joe—"

He held up a hand. "All of that notwithstanding, remember that you're highly valued around here, not just by me but by upper management. We won't let this affect your career, Tim. You have my word about that."

Despite his intention to stay calm, Tim was becoming agitated. "Honestly, Joe, I'm in shock. I've done my best to be a model employee here. And whatever I said to whoever it was, I certainly didn't mean anything by it."

He nodded. "I know. And you are a model employee. But in an organization as large as Hark—even a privately held one—the lawyers and the bureaucrats all have to keep busy. No matter what you meant by whatever you said, what's important now is how she *felt* about it. But you'll emerge from this without a trace. I'm make sure of that." He gave Tim a weak smile and then continued, "Now, I can't stop the system from going forward once a complaint is lodged with HR. One hasn't been yet, but if it is, it has to be processed. Hopefully, that won't happen. I'll try my best to prevent it."

Tim's shoulders slumped. He had two feelings deep in his gut that he despised—powerlessness and vulnerability. He bit his lip and waited.

"Look," Joe said. "Between you and me, and this is completely off the record"—he motioned, locking his lips before continuing—"a majority of these women are overly sensitive. Used to be, they were happy to have a job and they didn't complain. A lot of them quit when they started having kids—but not all." He grimaced. "The ones that stayed were the serious career women, and they were as ambitious as you are. But they knew how to get ahead and how to get along. Not anymore, though." He clasped his hands and leaned forward. "Now, any female employee can get upset about something extremely minor and then go on the warpath trying to get a good man fired. Every time, I've done my best to keep that from happening while what I really wanted to do was get rid of the woman."

Tim continued to keep silent.

Joe cleared his throat. "That said," he continued, "this situation isn't as bad as that. But we need to take care of this and nip it in the bud. We don't want it going to HR or anything getting documented."

"Okay. What do I have to do, Joe?" Tim's stomach was in a knot.

"Meet with her, here in my office, with me present. Tell her you didn't mean to offend her."

"*Of course* I didn't mean to offend her—"

"And don't say anything else, Tim. Just do what I'm telling you, and this will go away." He paused for a second and then added, "Trust me."

As Tim trudged back to his office, he felt numb and afraid, and he couldn't help but glance at all the secretaries. He'd been polite with all five and often told them he was appreciative of their work. He'd tried to be nice, not only to them but to everybody. He had complimented many of them on their appearance and certainly hadn't meant to upset anyone. Well, that would never happen again. As for his remarks about Roger, the idea that someone had complained about what he said stung.

But Tim *had* to trust Joe about this, even though Joe's words kept reeling in his brain. He didn't really know Joe, but they had gotten along fine over the past year for two reasons. Number one, Tim produced for him. And number two, Tim accepted him for who he was at the office—candid and often brusque. Joe wasn't into feelings, which was fine, but Tim could see how he might think that some people—women—were oversensitive, to put it mildly. For all Tim knew, Joe might have gotten called on his own behavior toward women in the past.

Ever since that night at Max's house when the Riverfest had become the topic of conversation, Tim had the impression that Joe was a bit of a snob too. He didn't care for the riffraff—"the great unwashed," in his words—and his tone had seemed condescending, if not arrogant. He had to take Joe at his word that he would support him in this situation, but now he wondered what kind of man Joe really was.

Is he the kind who could kill a woman? Is he a criminal—or even a monster?

Tim returned to his office, sat down at his desk, and ran a hand through his hair. *What's the matter with me? It's just as likely—or unlikely—that the Barbie Killer is someone who works at Hark as someone who works anywhere else. Or doesn't work at all. Joe's a Midwesterner, old-school and maybe a bit of a misogynist. But he's not a murderer.*

Is he?

———●———

"Since when is paying someone a compliment offensive?" Dolly asked that night.

Tim lifted his arms to his sides, palms up. "I have no idea. Since now, I guess. Or before now, and I didn't get the memo."

She sat on the bed while Tim changed out of his work clothes. "What's her name? And why was she so upset when she heard you say that?"

"Joe wouldn't tell me. And I don't know. It had nothing to do with her. Joe said to stick to topics about work and work only. Which I almost always do and always have done."

"Well, it sounds like bullshit," she said, leaning back on her elbows. "I'm glad he said he's in your corner."

"Yeah," Tim said. "Hopefully, he wasn't lying. Anyway, I'm supposed to tell her that I didn't mean to offend her and then she'll drop it. According to Joe."

"When are you meeting with this woman? Tomorrow?"

"I don't know." He sat down beside her on the bed. "Listen. Let's stop talking about it, okay? I just need time to process it so I can get it out of my mind and get a good night's sleep."

"Okay. I love you."

"I love you too," he said and gave her a kiss. "Now, let's go downstairs, and I'll pour us both a drink before dinner, okay?"

<hr>

The next morning, Joe called Tim into his office at nine o'clock. He was at his desk when Tim walked in. Tamara Weeks sat in one of two chairs across from Joe.

"Good morning," Tim said.

Tamara gave Tim a side glance, barely turning her head. Her lips were pursed.

"Have a seat, Tim," Joe said.

Tim sank into the other chair and waited, feeling tense. He was shocked that it was her and thought they had gotten along fine in the past.

"Now then," Joe continued, "let's get to the point of this meeting. Tamara, as I said earlier, I advised Tim of your feelings about his comments and, specifically, his choice of words recently. He requested that we meet so that he could offer you an apology."

I'm supposed to apologize to her for making an innocent remark and for using words that somehow hurt her feelings? Despite knowing he had no choice but to do so, Tim set his jaw and pressed his tongue against the roof of his mouth. *How am I ever going to know what might offend her in future—or anyone else, for that matter?*

He looked at Joe then turned to Tamara. Tim felt like his face was a gray rock. "I didn't mean to offend you, and I'm sorry if I did."

She stared at him without blinking, her expression icy. "*If* you did? Rest assured, you did." She turned to Joe, cocked her head, and crossed her arms in front of her.

"I'm sure Tim meant to say *that*, not *if*. He is sorry *that* he offended you. Right, Tim?" He gave Tim an expectant look, his eyebrows raised.

Tim's ears were getting hot. "Y-yes," he stammered, looking at neither of them. Then, with effort, he turned to Tamara, took a breath, and resolved to speak in a measured tone and to sound as sincere as possible. "I am deeply sorry that I offended you. I apologize for having done so."

There.

Tamara shook her head ever so slightly, as if she thought Tim was just another boorish man she had to put up with at the office. "Fine. I accept your apology." She looked at Joe. "I withdraw my complaint and don't need to have it go any further than this room."

"Excellent," Joe said a little too happily. "I mean, I know that Tim is grateful to you for withdrawing it. I appreciate it, too, and agree with keeping things between us in this instance. Anytime we resolve an issue ourselves, it's better for all concerned."

Tamara said nothing for a moment. "I'm not so sure about that, Joe. However, I've made my decision." She turned to Tim. "But it better not happen again."

"Oh, it won't," Joe assured her, throwing Tim a cautionary look that seemed to mean *stay still and be silent*. He did. "That's all then, Tamara. Have a good day."

Joe stood, and Tamara and Tim rose. Without another word, she walked out and shut the door behind her.

Joe put his hand on Tim's shoulder. "That could have gotten ugly. Thank God it didn't."

"Joe—"

"Shake it off," he said. "It's over, and no harm's been done." He looked at the door and then back at Tim. "She's just one of many bitchy women I can't get rid of. For now anyway. But don't worry. Eventually, I will. Trust me." He smiled and waved Tim off. "Back to the grindstone, eh?"

Tim nodded and headed down the hall toward his office, deep in thought but trying to look normal. He kept his mouth shut and his expression neutral, not a grimace or a scowl.

He didn't know which was worse, the weak feeling of walking down the hall with his tail between his legs or the stunned feeling in his gut about Joe's declaration.

Chapter 37

A few minutes later, Tim called Dolly from work.

"Everything's okay now," he said. "I apologized, and she withdrew her complaint. No probation, no nothing."

"Who was it?"

"Her name is Tamara Weeks."

"It's over, though, right?"

"I guess. I hope so. Actually, it is. Don't worry."

"I won't if you don't."

"I won't," he said. "I'm going to let it go and chalk it up to the unfairness of life. And to working for a big corporation. *And* to working for Hark. In any case, I'll be watching everything I say around here, effective immediately."

"Good."

"I better hang up now. Don't want to be eavesdropped on again. See you tonight, sweetheart."

Dolly glanced at the clock. It was time to pick up the kids at school, and as she drove the short distance, she tried to put herself in Tamara's place. She believed that Tim hadn't tried to offend her, but you never knew what really went on inside someone else's head. That said, she hoped he would never have a similar issue at the office again. Nothing like it had ever happened in Atlanta, perhaps because people were generally friendlier there. But this was how things were now, and Tim had learned a lesson he wouldn't forget. At least all he'd had to do was apologize. Working at Hark company headquarters was supposed to be a positive for his career, but this episode made it feel more like a negative.

Dolly was on the way to her therapy session with Clarice the next day when she realized she was being followed.

A dark-blue sedan was right behind her as she drove down Web Road, and the driver, a man, kept making every turn that she did. At first, she didn't think it was odd. Huntington was a small town after all. And with its perpendicular, grid-like four-lane roads, there wasn't only one shortest route to a destination, but there was normally one route that most people took. In a minute, this guy would go his own way to wherever he was going.

But he stayed behind her and right on her butt. She began driving under the speed limit in the right lane, hoping he'd pass her on the left, but he didn't.

Did I do something to piss him off? Maybe he's just a jackass. There's road rage in Kansas too. Go around me, whoever you are.

He didn't, and her pulse quickened, and she started to panic. Had she seen that car before, and if so, where? She kept glancing at the driver in her rearview mirror. He had a dark-colored ball cap on and wore sunglasses. Something about his jawline looked familiar.

When she needed to turn left, she waited until the last second to change lanes and didn't use her turn signal. He stayed on her tail.

Then she veered off the route to Clarice's office, taking several turns this way and that. Each time, he followed. Once or twice, he briefly let a car in between them but still managed to stay behind her. She racked her brain, trying to remember if she had seen him before and where. Was he someone who worked at Ardennes or at the Athletic Club? Was he the husband of a friend or neighbor? Whoever he was, she'd seen him *somewhere.*

Think.

Beads of sweat were forming on the back of her neck. This wasn't happening by chance. He was following her because he wanted to confront her. Why?

She tried in vain to calm down. She would be at Clarice's office in moments. As she entered the parking lot, she prayed that he would keep going.

But he turned into the lot and followed her as she drove slowly around looking for a parking place. She didn't want to get out of the car, but she wanted this to stop, and she didn't want to drive home and lead him there. She found a parking place sandwiched between a line of other cars that was close to the building and whipped into it. He passed behind her. There were no other empty spaces nearby.

She grabbed her purse and locked the car before she ran inside the building. The concierge waved at her as she rushed to the elevator. The door opened, and she quickly stepped inside and pushed the button for the fourth floor.

The door shut, and she heaved a sigh of relief. Then she trembled. *What if he came into the building right behind me and is watching to see which floor I'm stopping on? What if he took the stairs and is standing there when the elevator door opens?*

Before she had time to push another button, the door opened on Clarice's floor to an empty hallway. Dolly scurried to her office, opened the door, and shut it behind her. She was shaking.

"What's going on, Dolly?" Clarice put her arm around her and led her over to a club chair. "Did you get another note?"

Dolly took a deep breath. "No. A man just followed me all the way here."

"Are you certain?"

"Yes," she said. She described exactly what happened and said she had gotten a glimpse of the driver and thought she had seen him before.

"Did you get the license plate number?"

She shook her head. "I ran inside so fast that I didn't see it."

"Okay, let's not panic. He was driving erratically and aggressively, but you're safe now, and nothing happened to you."

"What if he was the person who left the notes? He knows my car. Maybe he's been watching me like he said and he knew I was coming here today. Maybe he knows everywhere I go and where I live. What if he's waiting for me right now?"

What if he's the killer?

Clarice picked up the phone. "I'm going to have a security guard escort you to your car and a policeman follow you home when we're done today."

Chapter 38

He pulled into his driveway, parked in the garage, and walked over to the shed. His wooden box was sitting where it belonged right next to his workbench. He reached down to open it but stopped himself.

Something is off in here. Something is out of place.

He looked around and surveyed the tools hanging on the wall. He kept each one in a specific place. His father had taught him early that you had to put things back where they went and keep them organized. It was one of the few things he'd learned from the man. "Everything has a home," he had said countless times.

Something is not in its home.

Then his eyes rested on an empty spot in the corner. One of his hammers should have been hanging there. Someone must have come out here and taken it. His wife or one of his kids?

But that didn't make sense because they didn't go into his shed. They didn't use any of his tools, and they knew he stored them and his weapons there. He unlocked the wooden box, tossed the new dolls inside, and locked it. That night, he casually mentioned the missing hammer to his wife, certain that she would say that she didn't have it.

He was wrong. She said that indeed she'd gone out to the shed that very day to look for something to defend herself with in case the Barbie Killer broke in and attacked her. Thinking he wouldn't miss it, she had taken the hammer and assumed he wouldn't mind. He did, of course, but instead of saying so, he gently assured her that she didn't need it and that he would protect her. The next day, he put it back where it belonged.

He was in panic mode because he couldn't find the key to his wooden box.

He almost always kept the antique brass key in his wallet, but sometimes, he slipped it into his pocket. He checked each of his pairs of pants and didn't find it but found two pockets with holes in the seams. Had the key slipped out? When had he worn those pants, and where had he been? If one of the kids found the key, they wouldn't know what it opened. If his wife had found it, she might know.

What if she'd noticed his box in the shed and had gone out there and unlocked it?

If she had, well, then he would know by now, he told himself. She would have confronted him or at least begun acting differently around him. She hadn't done either. But she might be a better actress than he realized. If she had seen what was in the box, he might have to make sure she could never tell anyone. There was only one way to do that, and he didn't know if he could. But for a moment, he let his mind travel there because fantasy was a lot less dangerous than reality.

There were all kinds of ways people could die accidentally. They could drown, or choke, or be poisoned. They could die in a fire. He could make that happen without anyone suspecting him, and then he would mourn her death like any grieving husband would. But he didn't want his children to grow up without a mother.

She was out somewhere with them now and wouldn't be back for hours. He searched every nook and cranny in each room of the house, and the key was nowhere to be found. Then he went through his car, the shed, and the entire yard. No dice. He could break open the box, but then he would have to replace it, something he didn't want to do.

Or he could replace the lock.

He wasn't a locksmith, but it couldn't be that hard. There was an antique hardware supplier down in Bonneville where he could buy a replacement bit and a barrel key exactly like the missing one. It was a skeleton key, long and skinny with a loop on one end and a perpendicular flag on the other. He would have to file the flag down with his Swiss file. Once he did, it would fit the post in the current lock and he could open the box with it. If nothing in it had been disturbed, that didn't mean it hadn't been opened, though.

He set aside those concerns for now, moved the heavy box to his car using a dolly, and heaved it into the trunk. Then he drove to Bonneville and found what he needed. When he got home, he took the box back to the shed and got to work.

He made the replacement key, unlocked the box, and examined its contents. Everything had been tossed about during the trip to and from Bonneville and lay about willy-nilly. He rifled through his souvenirs to make sure everything was accounted for. The ones from his early missions were in the bottom, and none of them were missing. He fingered the photos and IDs of the later ones, up to the mission back in 1988. He sorted through the ones from his recent missions and then started. The items he'd brought home from his latest mission weren't there. *Don't panic.*

He breathed in deeply, took another good and careful look, and discovered her driver's license and business card wedged against the side at the bottom. He let out a sigh of relief.

Then he removed the lock, installed the new one, and made a new key to fit it. The fear that someone in his family had seen the contents of his box gnawed at him, though.

Over the next few days, he watched the way his wife behaved like he never had before. There was definitely a chance that she knew his secrets and might even turn him in. Had he been too brusque when she went out to the shed to get that hammer? Had his reaction bothered her and piqued her curiosity about what he stored there?

What was that fable about women and curiosity? The story of Pandora's box with all of the world's evils stored inside? About how women couldn't resist opening a box, even—especially—if they'd been warned not to?

If she had found the original key *after* he'd replaced the lock and made the new key, he was safe. Concealed from his own wife. As always.

But if she had found and used it before then, she would know his real identity and would be acting strangely around him. There was no doubt about that. She would be treating him very differently. He had to think everything through and not jump to any conclusions. He ought to just ask her about it and gauge her reaction. If she acted normal, then all was well. If she didn't—if she was nervous, or distracted, or just not herself—he would know.

Somehow he would figure this thing out and get to the bottom of it.

Because his life might very well depend on it.

Chapter 39

Tim and Dolly firmly believed that the guy who had tailed her to Clarice's office was the same one who had written the notes, who was watching her, and who could be stalking her. If he wasn't the Barbie Killer, then he was another deranged and possibly violent man. Either way, Dolly was in danger. But both she and Tim felt sure that he was the killer.

Tim had just gotten very good news from one of the headhunters he had been in contact with. Three employers were interested in him, and all were located on the East Coast—Charleston, Jacksonville, and Miami. Each company was midsize or larger, and the salary was competitive with what he earned at Hark. Tim said that flying out to interview with them and leaving Dolly home alone right now was out of the question, so the recruiter asked for phone interviews, and all three employers consented. If any of them later requested a follow-up meeting in person, then Tim and Dolly would take the kids out of school, and she and they would go with him.

Meanwhile, Dolly was focused on trying to understand the killer and on gleaning clues about his behavior and how it had changed. Decades ago, he hadn't broken into his victims' homes. Evidently, they had let him in when he knocked on their doors and apparently posed as a someone who needed to make a phone call. Dolly had read that was how he entered the home of the victim whose boyfriend survived. His other victims' homes had shown no signs of forced entry either. He hadn't broken into Maggie's hotel room, but he did break into Dana's house.

Also, in the past he'd been meticulous and very careful. He'd even learned from the one blunder he'd made when he left that boyfriend for dead rather than making sure that he was. He had been sure to choose women who were home alone after that. He was very patient as well, often spacing out his murders over months or years. Lately, though, he seemed to be on a killing spree. He wasn't just taking more chances than before, either. Now he was acting brazenly. Instead of staying hidden in the shadows, he'd chosen to frighten and threaten Dolly in broad daylight, in public.

Dolly knew he was crazy. He had to be mentally ill to be able to do what he did. But now, he almost seemed delusional and unhinged, even for a murderer. Apparently, he thought he was smarter than the authorities and that he would always be able to elude them.

It might be a long shot, but maybe he actually *was* the person who had killed the teenage girl in the sixties, and she had been his first victim. There was no real indication to suggest it, but Dolly decided to allow her mind to consider the possibility anyway.

At the time, he would have been a teenager. He might have known the girl and could have slashed her throat in a fit of rage with his knife. Or he might have stalked her for weeks and planned to kill her that way. Then again, her gruesome and grisly murder was quite different from the spotless and usually bloodless ones known to be committed by the Barbie Killer. Although he had stabbed a couple of his victims—as well as one victim's boyfriend—none of those wounds were fatal, and they were probably unplanned.

But if he murdered that girl by cutting her throat, maybe the sight of so much blood had caused him to develop hemophobia, which might have prompted him to find another way to kill. It might be unlikely, but it was possible, and Dolly wasn't ready to dismiss the idea. Yet.

Chapter 40

He had to prove to himself once and for all that no one in his family had found the key and opened his box before he had changed the lock. Over the last few days, he'd been taking note of everyone's mood and demeanor, and no one had been acting strange. But that wasn't enough.

He could ask his wife and kids straight out if they had seen an odd-looking old key lying about. It was an innocent question, and posing it was a risk he ought to take. He hadn't been able to yet, however. Maybe one of them had found it but hadn't opened the box and would just hand the key over to him if he asked them for it.

No one at home had mentioned it. His wife had been her usual self, and now, he felt certain she hadn't come across it. Was it just his imagination, or had his children been behaving strangely lately? He needed to know what they knew or thought they knew.

Before he asked any of them about the key, there was one more thing he ought to do. Each time he opened his wallet, he always felt for it to confirm that it was behind his cash. Where had he been the last time he did that before he realized it was gone? Maybe it fell out of his wallet when he paid for his lunch at work. He had already checked Lost and Found, and no one had turned it in. Maybe he dropped the key in a store or at the barbershop. But he hadn't gotten a haircut recently, and his wife did the grocery shopping and all the other errands.

He drove around town, trying to jog his memory about where he'd gone recently.

Then he remembered that he'd gone to the gas station nearest his home the other day. Maybe the key was sitting on the ground next to one of the pumps. He didn't like to draw attention to himself, but he would if he had to. He drove to the station and pulled up to one of the gas pumps but didn't see it on the ground. After he filled his tank, he walked around near the other pumps but found nothing. Then he went into the mini-mart to pay and asked the clerk if anyone had picked up an old-looking key.

"What does it look like?" the guy at the register asked.

He described it and added that it opened a trunk that his wife's mother had given her.

The clerk opened a drawer and pulled it out. "Is this it?"

He nodded. "Thank you. Who turned it in?"

"Some woman did. She said she meant to when she found it but forgot to."

"When did she find it? Did she say?"

"I don't remember, man. Sorry."

———◉———

The possibility that that woman, whoever she was, could have seen him drop the key, figured out where he lived, and then used it to unlock his box—not to mention going back to the gas station and turning in the key afterward—was *extremely* slim. Even so, the idea that he could be identified, arrested, and sent to prison for life—or worse—weighed heavily on him. If he knew that was about to happen, he might have to take his own life.

Just thinking about suicide made him sick. It was the coward's way, and he abhorred cowards. And it would destroy his wife and children. They thought he was a good man, and he was one. It was just that he did bad things.

If he were captured, though, the dilemma he would face would be an example of Hobson's Choice—when you were forced to choose one of two alternatives, neither of which were desirable. He had learned the term when he was in the service. He couldn't count the number of times back then when he'd faced two very bad choices and had had to choose one.

He wouldn't choose to kill himself, though. If the police caught him and a jury convicted him, he would go to prison, and eventually he would be executed. In a way, that would be a blessing. He would be able to stop doing this for good and could finally get relief from the demons. They couldn't control him any longer or make him do their bidding. He could stop living a double life, stop being the Barbie Killer, and just be himself. The same man, yet totally different, and free.

But his wife and children would abandon him. Nobody would mourn him.

Is it my destiny to die without being mourned by those I love?

He couldn't bear the thought.

Chapter 41

After they had visited the victims' homes and she got the second creepy note, Dolly told Heidi about both of the notes. The day after she'd been followed, she had called Heidi and told her about that too. That week, she and Tim traded cars. Since then, she'd been keeping her eyes peeled for dark-blue sedans, and so had he. Now that she was looking for them, they seemed to pop up everywhere, but she didn't see the person who had tailed her behind the wheel or anywhere else in town. She was back to driving the minivan now, and if he followed her again, she planned to drive straight to the police department.

Today, she decided to tell Heidi about her theory that the Barbie Killer had cut the teenage girl's throat when he was a boy and had subsequently changed his MO because he couldn't stand the sight of blood.

"It's really just a hunch," Dolly said when they talked on the phone, "and I'd dismissed the idea that he killed her even though I hadn't forgotten it. But I think there's a reason why his MO is what it is, and why he strangles women and doesn't use a gun or a knife."

Heidi knew what Dolly's phobias were, and she had told Dolly she was claustrophobic and didn't ride in elevators alone because she was afraid of getting stuck.

"I get what you're saying," Heidi said. "Then again, maybe he strangles simply because blood is evidence and he doesn't leave evidence behind."

"Good point."

"Then again, you might be on to something."

"Well, like I said, it's just a hunch at this point. I've been racking my brain about him, though, and about how and why he does what he does. The only other thing I've come up with is that he seems to be taking more chances now than he did earlier, like breaking into a house instead of just ringing the doorbell like he used to do. And if he's the guy who followed me and who wrote those notes, he's not afraid to risk being seen anymore."

"*If*," Heidi said. "But let's pray that he's *not* the guy who wrote them and that the person who did is just some punk."

"Well, whoever wrote them, I do believe that the Barbie Killer thinks he's invincible, and I think he's not as risk averse as he used to be. But he must have a weakness, and if it's not a phobia of blood, it might be that he's convinced he's a genius."

"So what do we do about that?"

"Outsmart him," Dolly said. "Look, he may *be* very intelligent. That doesn't mean he isn't neurotic. He's probably paranoid, too, and we know he's deranged. At some point, he's going to mess up big time. Because what goes around, comes around."

"I hope you're right about that," Heidi said. "How do we outsmart him, though?"

"We stay one step ahead of him and try to figure out what he's going to do next and what mistakes he might make. We track him down without ever having to confront him so the police can arrest him before he kills anyone else."

Chapter 42

He had decided to start with Heidi. Over the weekend, he would plan how to do it. He could go to her house while she was out, get in without anyone knowing, and wait for her.

The following Wednesday, he was ready. She had a hair appointment that day at noon. Her daughter had gymnastics right after school, one of her sons had basketball practice, and the other ran cross-country. Nobody would be home until at least six o'clock. If she didn't come straight home after getting her hair done, he would wait for a while. If she didn't return in time for him to act, he would come back another day when he could leave work again.

Heidi's backyard was enclosed by a wood fence—the gate was unlocked—and the house behind this one had tall trees. Well, tall for Kansas. He'd had no trouble getting into the place through a window well in the basement. No one had seen him arrive.

He'd been waiting for over an hour when she walked in the door.

His pulse quickened. He breathed in slowly and exhaled, making no sound. He was wearing a dress shirt and dress pants—not business attire but the kind of ensemble he would wear to church—and had his sleeves rolled up to his elbows. He stood in the dining room against the wall, hidden behind heavy floor-to-ceiling draperies. He had placed the doll and his Polaroid camera on the floor next to him. They could stay there until he needed them. Unlike the Garner home, this one didn't have an open floor plan. All the rooms were divided by walls, and the dining room wasn't off the kitchen. You had to walk down a short corridor and pass a half bath to get there.

That was where she was. He could hear her in there, putting down her purse and opening a can of pop. That would be a Diet Coke, he decided. She drank a lot of them.

Before she left the kitchen, he had to move.

He slowly pulled a pair of dark-tan pantyhose from his pocket and pulled it over his head. Then he emerged from behind the draperies. Quiet as the grave, he crept across the room and down the hall. He peered into the kitchen. She was standing next to the sink with her back to him.

Perfect.

He would seize her around the neck with his gloved hands. She would be completely surprised and would struggle, but he was ready. He would keep her in an iron grip as she sputtered and as her strength waned. It would take a minute or two. Strangling a woman took a lot more time than people thought it did. It wasn't like in the movies.

When he was done, he would leave her in the kitchen. He wouldn't bother with her clothes or take time to do anything else to her today. The authorities would wonder why he hadn't, which would amuse him. He would put the Barbie doll next to her body, take a photo of it, and leave the photo, the way he always did. He would take whatever he wanted from her purse to keep as souvenirs and then get out the way he got in. No one would ever be the wiser. Then he could shift his focus to Dolly and do whatever the demons demanded of him. It was time. She was the true mission, the one he would spend time torturing. This nosy, loud woman was only an obstacle keeping him from her.

He stepped lightly into the kitchen, stopping just behind her, and reached for her neck. Just as his fingers closed on it, his foot slipped on something, and he lost his balance. In the moment it took to right himself, she whirled around, screamed, and slashed the underside of his forearm with a knife.

He freaked out. In shock, he grunted in pain and held his arm tightly against his body. He couldn't believe she had wounded him. She was facing him now, gripping the kitchen knife and pointing it at his face. Her eyes were wild, and he staggered backward, trembling. There was a bowl of diced potatoes and a cutting board on the counter behind her. He'd slipped on a potato peel on the floor.

What an idiot I am not to have brought my gun.

His arm throbbed. Had she hit a vein? Even if not, he had to abort and run away. Now.

He leapt over to the sliding glass door on the other side of the table. He opened it, ran outside, and then walked around the side of the house, pulling the pantyhose off his head and stuffing it in his pocket. His mind raced. He trotted around to the street, walked two houses down and to his car, which was parked around the corner. He climbed inside, willing himself to calm down.

His mind flashed back to the one other time when things hadn't gone as planned. It was back in the 1980s when that woman's boyfriend somehow survived after he stabbed him in the gut. When the guy began to bleed profusely, he had left him for dead and focused on the woman. But it was a big mistake. He had been too quick with the woman and had left without making sure the man was dead. Unfortunately, the guy had passed out and held on until the paramedics arrived. But the boyfriend wasn't able to describe him, so the cops had nothing to go on.

Since then, he had always worn the pantyhose. He felt sure that Heidi wouldn't be able to identify him. But she was still living and breathing on this earth. She hadn't been eliminated.

The whole thing was a big failure.

Sitting behind the wheel, he examined his arm. The gash was long but not deep. He wasn't going to die. He grabbed his first aid kit from the glove box and covered his wound with two large bandages and wound some gauze around them.

He wiped his hands and scratched his jaw as he looked around. He saw no one. If someone had been looking out the window and saw him, he might be screwed. Or not. People didn't like to get involved, and Midwesterners weren't known for poking their noses where they didn't belong. Chances were, if someone had spotted him, they hadn't given it a thought. Besides, in public, the only thing he'd been guilty of was walking fast.

But she had surely called the cops by now, and they would be here any minute. He started the car and drove slowly out of the neighborhood, turning left onto Web Road. When he got home, he would force himself to clean his wound and then make sure it healed properly and didn't get infected.

Why didn't I see the knife in her hand, and why didn't I grasp it immediately and take it away from her? Even if I cut myself in the process?

He'd meant to surprise her, yet she had surprised him. He'd gotten cocky, and it had cost him. If she hadn't had that knife and used it on him, she would be dead right now.

Then he slapped his forehead in frustration. He'd left the doll and camera on the dining room floor behind the drapery. But it wasn't like he'd had the time to snatch them up. Even so, this was the first time he had ever left anything at the scene.

His fingerprints weren't on them. He always wore gloves when he handled them. And before he took them to a mission, he wiped them down, just to be sure. You could never be too careful.

But when the cops found the doll and the camera, they would know it was him. She would tell them she had cut him and where. The press would report it, and he would be hunted down like he had never been before.

⎯⎯⎯●⎯⎯⎯

An hour later, he delicately removed the bandages and took a look at his arm. It wasn't bleeding anymore, and the wound had closed up. It wasn't deep, but it was ugly, and it throbbed a little, so he took some Tylenol for the pain. He probably needed stitches, but seeing a doctor was out of the question. He cleaned his wound and put iodine on it, grimacing at the sting, and then put on new bandages.

As long as he kept it covered and hidden—and it didn't get infected—he would be okay. It would heal. He couldn't let his wife see it, but in case she did, he needed a cover story. Maybe he would say he'd done it in his shed when he reached for a tool without noticing that a knife was underneath it, blade side up. But that was very unlike him, and she knew that he was careful. He had never injured himself in all their years together.

A more believable lie would be that he had tripped in the shed and cut his arm on a reciprocating saw blade. She didn't know one blade from another, so he didn't have to be specific. He'd told her time and again that he kept very sharp tools in his shed. He could say that he was lucky the cut wasn't deeper and assure her that there was no need for him to see a doctor because he'd had a tetanus shot last year.

But she would hear the news on television just like everyone else. So the best plan was to hide his wound while it healed. There would be a scar, but maybe he could explain that away later, saying he'd always had it and expressing surprise that she never noticed it. Or he'd make something else up. It didn't matter. It wasn't a very good plan, but it was all he had at the moment. In any case, he had to hide it, not just from her but from everybody because he couldn't risk the consequences of not doing so.

Meanwhile, he had to plan and execute his next move so that he could satisfy the demons. His failed attempt to eliminate Heidi had changed everything, and now, things had really gotten out of hand. It might result in him being caught—and soon. He had passed the point of no return, and he couldn't waste time waiting for his wound to heal properly.

He needed to go ahead and kill Dolly, and soon, while he still had the chance.

Chapter 43

The lead story on the local news was the Barbie Killer's foiled attack on Heidi Barron. The police chief said the perpetrator had a long cut on the underside of his forearm and that hospitals, doctors, and even veterinarians had been instructed to alert the police department if a man came in and asked them to treat such a wound.

According to the reports, Heidi hadn't heard him break in. When she felt his hands close around her neck, she reacted without thinking and didn't have time to panic. The chief said that she'd had a fight-or-flight response, and since her brain knew that she had a weapon in her hand, it chose to fight. Police officers arrived in minutes and put up a perimeter, but they had no luck. He was gone.

The cops searched the house and found a brunette Barbie doll and a Polaroid camera. There were a few drops of blood on the kitchen floor, but no blood was found outside. The Barbie Killer had vanished into thin air.

The next morning, Dolly called Heidi, who asked her to come over. Matt answered the door when Dolly arrived and ushered her into the house.

"Thanks for coming over," he said. "She's still in shock. I think we all are."

Heidi walked up behind him, and Dolly gave her a hug. "How are you?" she asked.

"I don't know," Heidi said, her tone uncharacteristically weak and hollow. Her face was pale and drawn. "It hasn't really sunk in, I guess."

"I'm sure it hasn't. You must feel so numb."

The two of them walked into the den and sat down on the sofa.

"I do. I keep on replaying it over and over in my head. I can't get it out of my mind. It's like a nightmare I can't forget." Heidi drew in a sharp breath and wiped away a tear. "God, I'm a mess."

"You can share anything you want—or not," Dolly said gently, taking her hand. "If you don't want to, that's okay."

"I do want to. I'm so glad you're here." Heidi looked her in the eye. "You know, visiting those victims' homes together and talking about him and why he does what he does—all of that felt so abstract. It didn't feel real. This was. Dolly, when he was standing right over there, inches away from me, in my kitchen, I felt completely helpless and powerless. It was awful."

"But something inside you made you do what you did. And without even thinking."

"That's right. I didn't think. I just acted." Heidi's eyes widened, and she shook her head. "I don't know how, though. When I saw the blood on his arm, I started shaking. And then I froze. I couldn't breathe. I thought he was going to grab the knife out of my hand and kill me right then. For some reason, he didn't, and I lived to tell the story." Heidi's eyes filled with tears. "I came this close to being his latest victim."

They hugged again, and after a moment, Dolly asked Heidi if she had seen what he looked like.

"No. He had pantyhose pulled over his head! I did notice that he was only a little taller than me, though."

"Maybe the blood will help the police. Did anyone in the neighborhood see him running away?"

"Not as far as I know. He must have jumped in a car and driven away before the cops got here. Dolly, it's so surreal."

"You must have really scared him—and badly wounded him too," Dolly said.

"That's just it," Heidi said. "I don't think I did. I mean, I didn't stab him or anything. Wish I had. All I did was slice his arm. As soon as I did, he went berserk and ran out of here."

"That is weird. But... are you thinking what I'm thinking?"

Heidi paused. "I'm thinking that your hunch might be right, that he could have a phobia of blood, and that seeing his own made him totally freak out."

"Me too," Dolly said. "Maybe the fear of blood is his Achilles' heel."

"If it is," Heidi said, "then it's what saved me."

On her way home, Dolly decided that instead of carrying only Mace and a gun in her purse, she was going to carry a sharp knife in it as well from now on. Just in case.

Because it was better to have one and not need it than to need one and not have it.

Chapter 44

Business attire was very good at hiding things like tattoos, scars, and fresh wounds.

At the office, most men—including Tim—didn't wear their suit jackets all day long. They put them on for meetings and consultations with clients, and when they took them off, they almost never rolled up their shirt sleeves. A white dress shirt might not conceal a bandaged wound on the underside of a forearm. But a shirt of any other color probably would. As Tim walked through the office, he couldn't help but notice who was wearing a white shirt and who wasn't.

Anyone who worked here could have a dark side and could be leading a hidden, private life. Serial killers lived on the fringes, though, and they probably weren't responsible men who worked hard to provide for their families. But perhaps this killer was the exception to the rule.

Whether he had a job or not—or a family—somebody was bound to notice his injury sooner or later. No medical professional had come forward saying they'd treated a man with such an injury, but Heidi had told Dolly that it wasn't a deep cut, so professional care might not have been necessary. The killer could be lying low and was probably pretty shaken up. Maybe he had even left town.

That was what Tim, Dolly, and the kids were doing tomorrow. Tim had face-to-face interviews scheduled over the next couple of days with two firms in Florida. He had told Joe that he needed to take some personal days off because he was going to the funeral of a family member there. Joe approved his request for time off, no questions asked.

Two days after Heidi thwarted the Barbie Killer's attack, she and Matt and their children went to Houston for a week.

The killer hadn't gotten his wish to make the national news, and Hark top management was grateful for that. If the police found him soon and picked him up, no doubt the networks would report it, but his brush with a Hark executive's family would be a small part of the story if it was included at all. Most people in the country weren't familiar with Huntington, Kansas, and even fewer knew that Hark was headquartered there. If the killer was arrested and sent to prison, the town's secret would be forgotten and its nightmare would be over. That was the best-case scenario. But if he managed to slip by the cops and killed once again, especially soon, the story could grow exponentially and might frighten people away.

Tim and Dolly didn't care, and neither did Matt and Heidi. Heidi had told Dolly that Matt was looking for a new position in either Houston or Charleston, South Carolina. Dolly had kept mum about Tim's job search, but once he found something, she would let her friend know. Right now, everything was uncertain. Matt was afraid the killer was angry at Heidi and might come back and be more prepared.

Tim, however, was convinced that the killer was one big step closer to murdering Dolly and that he would make sure he got the job done this time.

Chapter 45

The following Tuesday in the early afternoon, Dolly was at home alone.

He crept around the back of the house, slid down the window well, and broke in through a basement window. It didn't set off the security system because the doors were alarmed but the windows were not. They had to be hardwired to the system, so almost nobody had it done, and he already knew that they hadn't. He got inside the house easily, tiptoed to the foot of the stairs, and listened but didn't hear her. She must be doing something on the top level of the house, where all the bedrooms were. She would have to come downstairs eventually, though.

After what felt like an eternity, he heard her descending the staircase directly over him. When he walked up from the basement, the Berber carpeting on the stairs would muffle his steps. From down here, it sounded like she was milling around in the kitchen, opening cabinets and drawers. He would pick the right moment and then come upon her from behind.

He didn't relish the idea of leaving her children without a mother. But he didn't have a choice because he had to appease the demons. Maybe then they would leave him alone for good.

He crept slowly up the stairs. There was no door at the top, so when he got there, he crouched behind a corner at the far end of the den, a good twenty feet from the kitchen. From there, he could peer around it and watch her. She was standing at the island with her back to him, messing around with something. He would stay here for a few minutes and wait for the right moment.

She was fiddling with something, maybe doing some kind of craft or project. He had often seen her shopping at the local craft store. She seemed intent on what she was doing and unaware of anything else. Everything was going according to plan. It was best if she was distracted. That way, he could quietly approach her, twist her arm behind her back, and seize her around the neck.

Chapter 46

Dolly had risen early that day. After getting the kids to school and working out at the Athletic Club, she went to Dillons to buy groceries. When she walked to her car, she almost expected to find another note, but there wasn't one. At home, she cleaned the kids' bathroom and then organized her closet, setting aside clothes and shoes to donate. After that, she lay down to take a quick power nap before it was time to go pick them up at school. When she woke up, she was no longer in her bed.

She was standing in the kitchen, gasping for breath, and her throat was on fire.

Her right arm was pinned behind her, and she was clutching at the cord around her neck with her free hand. Terrified, she leaned forward, which only made the cord pull tighter. Someone was behind her trying to strangle her and was holding her right arm with one hand and squeezing the cord with the other. In vain, she tried to stomp on his feet. She kept struggling and started kicking her legs but couldn't break his grip. She could barely breathe, and her strength was rapidly fading.

Am I going to die? Or does he plan to let me live long enough to torture me and then *kill me? Should I try to stall by pleading and cooperating with him and hope I can get away?*

Her brain rejected all of that as her adrenaline level shot up. He was in control at the moment, but she wasn't going to let him win.

She was going to fight.

What was the right self-defense move to use if attacked from behind? She had no idea, and this was real, not practice. If she could somehow wrestle herself away from him, her arm could break. Dana's words popped up in her brain.

Getting injured is much better than dying.

She had a few seconds left. Then muscle memory she had developed from practicing the last moves Dana had taught her took over, and she stopped pulling away from him. A split second later, with all the strength she could muster, she snapped her head back against his head. She heard a loud crack as the back of her head exploded in pain.

But the cord had fallen from her neck, and her right arm was free now. Coughing and panting for breath, she turned around and faced him. There was a pair of pantyhose pulled over his head, and where his nose should be, a bright-red splotch was quickly spreading. Instead of hitting him, she froze.

"You bitch!" he yelled wildly as he came toward her.

She had made him bleed, and he was freaking out about it. She had to do it again. But not with her hands.

Out of the corner of her eye, she saw the solid pewter dish sitting on the counter and grabbed it. Without thinking, she knocked him hard in the face with it. He reeled back a step or two and staggered as more blood soaked through the pantyhose.

"Oh God!" he screamed. "Look what you did!" He covered his face with his hands.

She backed away and looked frantically around the room for her purse.

It was upstairs in her bedroom, and the gun and a knife were in it. The rest of the knives were in a knife block sitting on the counter to the right of the sink just behind him, so she couldn't reach it. A bottle of superglue and her Fiskars scissors were sitting on the island. She grabbed the scissors, closed both hands around the grip, and pointed them at him.

He lunged at her and, aided by the force of his movement and the little strength she had left, plunged the scissors deep into his abdomen.

Chapter 47

Searing, excruciating pain.

Dolly stood facing him, staring down at him. He was lying on the kitchen floor. She had popped him in the face with something. His nose was smashed, his face was bloody, and his gut was spurting more blood. The orange handles of a pair of scissors were sticking out of his belly. He was in agony, yet he was still alive. But he couldn't bear the sight of his own blood.

Was this really happening? Maybe it was only a nightmare and he would wake up any second, safe in his own bed.

But no. He could hear her talking. *Who is she talking to?* He couldn't answer even if he wanted to. He couldn't speak.

A long-ago image suddenly surfaced in his mind. A girl's body, covered in blood—like his was now? He'd hidden in the shadows while he watched the boy cut her throat that night, and he had kept mum about it all these years. He was very good at keeping secrets, and perhaps because of that, his mind had almost blocked the whole thing out. But deep in his consciousness, he knew things that he wished he didn't, and the consequences had been enormous.

The story that had gone around town afterward was embellished so many times that it took on a life of its own. Everyone believed that the killer was her boyfriend and had disappeared. The cops searched for him but couldn't find him and had never arrested anyone for the murder.

He'd heard what people said about that guy, though, and he heard the whispers. As was his wont, he'd been a good listener and a quiet observer. And he had hidden in the shadows and hadn't said a word about what he'd witnessed.

Ever since that night, he'd hated the sight of blood and had tried to avoid it. He preferred strangling. It took more time than slitting throats, but it was a lot less messy. Then the image of the body that he'd found that night flashed in his mind. It was hanging from a tree in the woods, a noose around its neck. The killer had been faced with Hobson's choice and had chosen to take his own life rather than be executed for what he'd done.

He'd cut down the body and buried it in a shallow grave. He never told anyone that or who the boy was because he'd decided that the boy's parents had been better off not knowing. Years later, the tree was chopped down, the field was cleared, and a new strip shopping center was planned for the site. A cement truck poured concrete over the makeshift grave while creating a large parking lot, which forever sealed the dead body underneath it.

The images left his consciousness as his pain intensified. He seethed in anger. Why hadn't he brought his chloroform or his pistol with him? He'd thought he wouldn't need them, that was why. Dolly wasn't as strong or knowledgeable about self-defense as her instructor had been. And holding a gun to her head hadn't seemed necessary because he'd thought that after attacking her from behind, he could overpower her within seconds and tie her up in less than a minute.

He would get up off the floor and make Dolly suffer and beg for mercy, and then he would kill her.

But he couldn't get up. He couldn't feel his limbs or move his head—or even his lips. It was all he could do just to breathe now. The pain emanated from his midsection, growing stronger with every second. He felt like he was bursting inside and collapsing at the same time. He lay there, waiting it out, willing himself to survive.

Chapter 48

She had watched him totter backward and fall to the floor. One of his legs twitched now, and blood spurted from his abdomen. He was making no sound.

She didn't touch him and did nothing to help him or to stop the bleeding. She grabbed the cordless phone and dialed 911.

"What's your emergency?" a voice asked.

"A man just tried to kill me, and I stabbed him!"

"What's your address, ma'am?"

With effort, she provided the information. Dolly was shaking, and her heart was beating faster than ever.

"Is the man dead?"

"I don't know! I don't think so. His leg was moving."

"Is it now?"

"I don't think so. Hurry!"

"EMS is on the way."

She hung up, called Tim, and told him what had happened.

"I'll be right there," he said.

She held on to the counter and willed herself to calm down while she waited. The whole time, she stared at the man. After an eternity, paramedics and cops suddenly appeared and filled the room.

"He's alive but fading," she heard an EMT say to someone.

A policeman approached her and stopped in front of her. "I need you to tell me what happened, ma'am. Start to finish."

Dolly gulped and rubbed the back of her head. There was a big bump on it, but she didn't feel any blood. She didn't know the whole story from start to finish. Between the time she had lain down to take a nap and the moment she felt her throat burning and his hands around her neck, she didn't know what happened or what she'd done. Obvious-ly, she had been sleepwalking. But it didn't seem to matter now.

"I'm a little shaky," she said, stalling. "Let me sit down somewhere."

"Sure."

The officer guided her into the den, and they sat down on the couch. EMTs were busy putting the man on a gurney, and cops swarmed around as two of the paramedics wheeled the gurney to the ambulance.

"Officer?" one of them called from the foyer. "We just found something. I think you're going to want to see it."

He nodded at Dolly and held out a hand. "Stay there. I'll be right back."

Just then, Tim rushed in the open front door, bounded over, and asked if she was okay.

Tears filled her eyes. "Yes. No. I don't know. I think they're taking him to the hospital. I don't think he's dead."

One of the paramedics came over, looked at Dolly's head, and of-fered to take her to the hospital to have it checked.

"No," she said. "I want to stay here with my husband. If I need to go to my doctor tomorrow, I will."

The police officer came back to the sofa. "Excuse me, sir?" he asked Tim. "Can I have a word with both of you, please?"

"With me, yes. My wife is a mess, though." He put his arm around her. "She's hurt, and she's in shock."

The officer was standing in front of them and looked as white as a sheet. "Yes, sir. Just want you to know that we know that he broke in-to the home and attacked her and that she stabbed him in self-defense. We just found a Barbie doll in his pocket."

"Are you saying—"

"We think he's the Barbie Killer, sir."

Tim called a neighbor and asked her to pick up the kids, and then he called the school. He took care of everything after that, including telling the kids what had happened. Dolly sat beside him, holding his hand, watching fear show on their young faces.

"Mom's okay," he said to them. "And the police caught him, thanks to her."

"Is he going to jail?" asked Cole.

Audrey had nestled in between her brothers and was holding her mom's other hand.

"He's in the hospital right now, but yes, he will," Tim said. "Mom has to go to the police station and tell what happened. I'm going to take her after we drop you guys off at the Barrons' house. We won't be long, and I'll call when we're on the way back to get you. Okay?"

Dolly hugged the kids and reassured them. When she and Tim got to the police station, she told the police she remembered doing something in the kitchen—she wasn't sure what it was now—and then she felt a man's hands grip her neck. On instinct, she had hit him with a heavy dish and then pointed the scissors at him when he lunged at her. The next thing she knew, he was on the floor.

"We've identified him," the policeman said, "and his blood type matches the blood that we found in the Barron home. We're searching his home right now."

"Who is he?" Tim asked.

"His name is Warren Grady."

Dolly gasped.

"You know him?"

"I met him once, and I know his wife, Lynn. She's a friend."

"Do you know him, too, sir? Or are you acquainted with him?"

"No," Tim said, "I'm not."

"Did he confess to the murders? And to killing Denise Hutchins back in the sixties?" Dolly asked.

"We questioned him in the hospital," the officer said. "But he said nothing and didn't confess to any of the homicides. We may find evidence in his home to tie him to the serial killings, but I don't know whether we'll be able to connect him to the cold case you mentioned. We may never know who killed her. I just learned that he died a few minutes ago."

Chapter 49

Warren Grady was the Barbie Killer.

He'd been an ordinary-looking man, with a square jaw and a nondescript face, and he had thin, dark hair. He was five foot ten, a hundred and seventy pounds, and forty-nine years old. He had a long scar on the underside of his left forearm from a recent wound. He worked as a residential and commercial technician for Mid-Continent Security Company, and he had been with them for ten years. Prior to that, he'd worked for the phone company for many years after serving in the army. He and his family were churchgoers, and his wife worked in the church office. Other than his time in the service, Grady had lived in Huntington all his life.

The police found an old manual typewriter in his shed that he'd used to type the envelope containing the note he sent to the newspaper. He'd also used it to type the notes Dolly had found on or in her vehicle. They found a locked wooden box in his shed and broke it open. Inside were a bunch of souvenirs of his murders—his victims' drivers' licenses, other personal items, and several Barbie dolls.

Reporters called the Garner home nonstop and waited outside for days. Eventually, Dolly talked to one who was with *The Huntington Post,* and the article was published on the front page. The story about the Barbie Killer and his death made the national news.

———◉———

Hark gave Tim as much time off as he wanted. The kids didn't go back to school until the following week, and when they did, the boys seemed ready—if not to talk to anyone about what had happened, to get on with their lives. And they were proud of Dolly for fighting off and stopping the killer.

Max and Glenda called, and so did Joe and Diane. Some neighbors—ladies from Dolly's book club—called too. All of them said that Dolly was a hero and very brave. Heidi and Matt came over that weekend and brought dinner.

"How are you doing, girl?" Heidi asked Dolly when they arrived that night.

"Pretty well," Dolly said, her face bright. "All things considered."

"Our wives are celebrities at Hark," Matt said, shaking Tim's hand. "Especially yours."

"She's a strong woman. They both are," Tim said. "And thank God this is behind them and all of us."

"She's not just strong, she's smart," Heidi said, cocking her head. "She knew to whip her head back and hit him with it while he had the cord around her neck. And she's been analyzing his behavior for some time and knew he would get freaked out by the sight of blood."

"I didn't know that for sure," Dolly said. "But luckily, he seemed to be. And it gave me time to grab the scissors." She shuddered. "I was lucky they were within my reach."

"Well, he flipped out when I cut his arm," Heidi said, "and I was lucky I had time to turn around and do it. Where was your purse, by the way?" She knew what Dolly carried in it.

Dolly shook her head. "Upstairs in our room." She looked at Tim and met his eyes for a second. They both knew why she hadn't taken it downstairs with her. "I had come down to the kitchen to fix a broken picture frame before leaving the house to pick up the kids."

It didn't seem necessary to add or explain that she'd been sleepwalking and when she had woken up. When Tim had seen the superglue on the island, he knew that was what happened because her phobia of it had vanished.

"Have the reporters stopped bugging you?" Matt asked Tim.

"For the most part, yes," Tim said. "Dolly's told the story of what happened over and over. Maybe soon, all four of us can move on from this."

Chapter 50

Six weeks later, Tim and Dolly closed on the sale of their house on a Friday morning.

That afternoon, they left town. Tim's new employer was paying for the move, including the transportation of one of their cars. So after the last box was loaded into the moving van, everyone climbed into the car to begin the journey to Florida, where Tim would start his new job the following week. When they'd told the kids that they were moving and where, all three of them clapped and cheered.

Dolly took one last look at the house before they drove off. Despite what had happened in it, they'd had no trouble selling it and had even made a profit. The buyers, who wanted an almost-new house, apparently weren't turned off by the history. And if it had ever had bad karma, perhaps the fact that Dolly stopped the killer there had transformed it into *good* karma.

She gazed out the window as they drove out of town. A thunderstorm was approaching, but they would soon be far enough away to avoid it. She idly wondered if it was the prelude to the approach of a tornado. She said a silent prayer of thanksgiving that they'd never encountered one. They planned to drive to Memphis, stay the night, and finish the trip tomorrow. When they arrived in Florida, they would check into a hotel and close on their new home the next day.

"How do you feel, babe?" Tim asked, smiling. All three kids were quiet, watching a videotape on a portable TV and videotape player that was positioned between the two front seats. "Happy to get out of town?"

"Thrilled," she said.

She would miss some of her friends here, and she would miss Heidi a lot. Matt had found a new job in Charleston, and they were moving next month. Heidi seemed as glad to be leaving Huntington as Dolly was. They had said an emotional goodbye just yesterday after a final lunch out together at Ardennes, promising to keep in touch and to visit when possible.

Tim grabbed Dolly's hand. "I can't believe how close I came to losing you."

She smiled weakly, her eyes suddenly teary.

"Won't be long 'til we're out of Kansas," Tim said.

"I never want to come back."

"We won't. I promise you."

Tim's new job sounded fantastic, and they were both excited about moving back to the east coast. She would have liked to live in Atlanta again, but she didn't mind letting go of that possibility once and for all. Their time in Atlanta, like their time in Huntington, was behind them, and a new adventure lay ahead. Tim's new company was based in Jacksonville, and they had found a beautiful home in a suburb, near good schools and close to the beach.

Once they got settled, Dolly might look for a part-time job. Or she might go back to school part-time and study criminal psychology and maybe train to become a criminal profiler. She had learned a lot about serial killers on her own, and she had been fascinated and intrigued by how and why they grew up to become monsters.

She breathed in deeply, feeling a mixture of contentment and satisfaction. She was ready to embrace the future, whatever it held. She glanced out the window, feeling wistful yet content. She wondered what Lynn's future would be like, and she regretted not having called her before leaving town. Instead, she had sent her a note expressing sympathy and wishing her healing and peace over the months to come.

"You're pretty quiet," Tim said. "What are you thinking about?"

"Lynn," she said. "I can't imagine what she's going through. She was terrified of the Barbie Killer."

"She must be in shock. Maybe she'll move away too." He threw her a glance and looked back at the road. "I've never been so happy to leave a company. Babe, if I knew when we moved to Kansas what I know now... if I could do it all over again—"

"Would you, Tim?"

He looked over at her again, his eyes serious and steady. "No, I absolutely would not."

Dolly squeezed his hand. "You know, the reason we didn't know what happened in Huntington before we arrived doesn't matter to me anymore. That's just the way it was. And we're leaving it a better place than it was when we got here."

"Do you still think our lot—or our house—was cursed?"

Dolly shook her head. "I was wrong. I don't think it had bad karma or that it brought us back luck. If anyone had to pay for what happened there so long ago, it wasn't us. It was the killer."

Acknowledgments

Several years ago, author Tim O'Mara asked me to contribute to the anthology *Down to the River*, a collection of crime stories taking place near an American river. Even though I'd never written a short story before, I consented and then considered where to set this one. I grew up in Atlanta, but the Chattahoochee was out because I hadn't lived near it. For a few months in college, I lived next to the Haw River where it flows south of Chapel Hill, N.C., but my memories of it are vague. Then, in the 1990s, my husband and I moved to Wichita, Kansas, through which the Arkansas River runs. During our time there, we took our kids to a yearly festival held near the riverbanks. Years later, I learned that a serial killer had lived in Wichita then and had been terrorizing the community for decades. My short story, *The Riverfest*, was set there, and although the characters' names are different and the setting is not Wichita but a fictional Kansas town, *The Barbie Killer* is an expansion of that story.

As I wrote it, the novel evolved and greatly improved with the help of much-needed feedback from fellow writers who are also my friends. Thanks go to Lee Ann Shobe, Katherine Hoehn, Linda R. Sexton, Jane Buyers, Chip Kirkpatrick, Jonathan Bryant, Marla McDaniel, Ned McCormack, and Ralph DeFalco. After I finished the manuscript and before I began searching for a publisher, my freelance editor, Laura Ownbey, helped me revise and polish it, and I thank her for her hard work, dedication, and encouragement.

I'm grateful to Lynn McNamee, owner of Red Adept Publishing, for believing in my novel and offering it a publishing home. Thanks go to my RAP content editor, Sara N. Gardiner, for her insights, suggestions, and commitment to helping me make the novel the best it can be.

Thanks also to my RAP line editor, Darlene Gardner, for her keen eye, attention to detail, and her spot-on suggestions. Since my protagonist's last name is Garner, I can't help but think that Sara and Darlene were meant to be a part of my story. I also thank author Erica Lucke Dean for her help and patience when I shared my thoughts and ideas for the book's cover.

Elen Christopher coined the killer's name, which became the title of this novel. At an Atlanta Celebrity Dance Challenge that I competed in, Heidi Barron won the right to have a character named after her. I hope you liked meeting Dolly's best friend in Huntington and your namesake, Heidi. I'm grateful to many friends, readers, and fellow authors in Georgia, Florida, and France who supported me and encouraged me as I wrote *The Barbie Killer*, including Wendy Lamb, Cheryl Swan, Fabienne Nicolas, and all my Read and Share members in Florida. Above all, thanks to my darling husband, Dennis, for believing in me, celebrating with me, and faithfully holding my hand along the way. *Je t'adore.*

About the Author

Julia McDermott grew up in Atlanta, graduated a year early from high school, and juggled two jobs waiting tables while earning degrees in Economics and French at the University of North Carolina. After spending ten months in the south of France, she moved to Texas, worked in finance and technology, and married her college sweetheart. While raising their four children—including a set of twins—she began her writing career.

Julia now lives in Florida, where she is a ballroom dancer and an active member of her local writing community. She is fascinated by the intricacies of the human mind, and when not writing or reading, she loves walking on the beach, traveling in France with her husband, and binge watching French and British murder mystery series.

Read more at https://juliamcdermottbooks.com/.

About the Publisher

Dear Reader,

We hope you enjoyed this book. Please consider leaving a review on your favorite book site.

Visit our site to find more quality books!

Read more at https://RedAdeptPublishing.com.